Tarantula Tide

Tarantula Tide

Sharon Tregenza

Kelpies

Kelpies is an imprint of Floris Books

This edition published in 2008 by Floris Books

The publisher acknowledges a Lottery grant from the Scottish Arts Council towards the publication of this series.

British Library CIP Data available

ISBN 978-086315-673-1

Printed in Poland

For Team Tregenza

Contents

1. Tammie norie

He looked like he wanted to kill me and *I* wanted to die. I was so embarrassed.

"Ye nasty little devil. You've thrown up all over my brand new racing boots."

"Sorry, I couldn't help ..." Another heave convulsed me and I jerked forward, grabbing my stomach.

"Agggh!" The massive biker leapt back in disgust.

"Jack, I've got them!" Mum rushed out on deck, waving a packet of sea-sickness pills.

With a menacing look in my direction the leather-clad giant turned away and clumped over to the other side of the ferry.

"You look terrible. Best get you into the cabin so you can lie down." Mum placed a cold hand on my forehead.

"I *feel* awful," I said. "This was a dumb idea. Who wants to go to Shetland anyway?" I puked the last of my meal over the side and, feeling weak and shaky, made my way to our cabin.

Near the staircase, a giant black and red boot was cradled in the lap of my victim, who was dabbing at the buckles with a handful of tissues, his beefy forearm tattooed with the name 'slasher' under the image of a dagger dripping blood.

Of all the people to chuck up on, I thought. I pulled my hood down to hide my face and crept past without him seeing me.

I took the sea-sickness pills and lay on the bed but the sea was swelling up and down outside the cabin window. I groaned and turned my face to the wall. "I'll never get to sleep." I moaned.

Mum woke me at seven the next morning.

Feeling headachy, the cold miserable morning didn't help. The buildings of Lerwick came out of the fog like blocks of giant Lego. Black rubber tyres lined the walls of the harbour. We threw our bags into the red Clio and waited our turn to drive off the ferry. I was relieved to hear the roar of a motorbike, which meant Slasher had left the boat.

We drove through mist, along the coast road and it was a while before I realized what was wrong with the hills and moors.

"There're no trees," I said.

Mum glanced up. "You're right. It looks almost moon-like, doesn't it? Stunning though. Look at all the little coves."

Turning off the road at last, we stopped and got out of the car. "What a pretty little cottage," Mum said in the voice she uses when she doesn't mean what she says.

I dragged my backpack and guitar case out of the boot, grunting. "It's a bungalow. It's just called *Oz Cottage*. It's not really a cottage at all."

Mum sighed. "We've got a week here, Jack. Let's enjoy it, shall we? It'll give us some time on our own. We need to talk about … what happened."

"I don't want to talk about what happened."

"You're going to have to sooner or later." Mum sounded as irritable as I felt. I took the heaviest case off her and heaved it onto my shoulder. It still surprised me how small my mother was. At twelve, I was already a good two inches taller. She passed me the key and I unlocked the door. The glass rattled in the frame. We stepped into a hallway with a red carpet and a plastic kangaroo on the wall. The house smelled damp.

"It's freezing in here."

"It'll soon warm up. That must be your room there. If you put your stuff in, I'll get the heaters on and make us a cup of soup."

My room had the same wet-leaf smell as all the other rooms. There wasn't much in the way of furniture: a bed with a blue duvet and a cupboard on either side; a mirror over another cupboard had a cartoon crocodile painted on it. There was some weird stuff on the walls too: a silhouette of a kangaroo on a yellow background with "CAUTION KANGAROOS CROSSING" written across it; two boomerangs, crossed like swords, were positioned near the window, and a hat with corks dangling down from the brim hung on the back of the door. It took me minute or two before I realized there was an Australian theme going on.

"Oh, I get it," I said. "*Oz* Cottage." On a shelf, a cross-eyed koala stuck its small pink tongue out at me.

I knelt on the bed. A pair of binoculars lay on the windowsill and I squinted through them out to sea. My mood changed immediately. We were just feet above the beach. Jagged rocks led out into the water where masses of birds fluttered and fought.

For a second I saw a dark head appear out of the waves, a seal?

"Coooool," I whispered and despite having promised myself I'd be miserable, I felt the first twinge of excitement.

"Soup's ready, Jack."

Mum must have found the heating. I could feel warmth coming from somewhere. She turned the radio on. She listens to Classic FM all the time. It drives me crazy. At home, in Edinburgh, I can listen to my music. I'm going to have my own band one day. I've started guitar lessons.

Mum handed me a mug and a packet of Doritos. The damp smell had gone and the house looked better with the lights on. The kitchen wasn't bad, tidier than our own anyway: shiny floors and worktops, and a fridge as big as a house. Mum saw me staring at it.

"Our loaf of bread and two pots of yoghurt look pretty silly in that," she said. "We'll do some shopping later." She checked her watch. "I don't know about you but I'm beat, what with the train to Aberdeen and that choppy crossing on the ferry. I'm off to bed for a few hours." She yawned and ruffled her hair. "I'm looking forward to this week, really I am."

"I'm not."

Mum sighed and put her hand to my cheek. I ducked away. *"Getoff."*

She stared hard at me for a few seconds, then shrugged her shoulders and said "Fine. See you later."

"I'm just going to go and check out the beach," I said. Mum nodded but didn't answer. Outside, the smell and sound of the sea was everywhere. Ours was one of only three houses on a short curve of road. It was so quiet; nothing but smooth green hills on one side, the sea on the other and the wind.

I plugged myself into my iPod and tucked it into my pocket. Pushing past a prickly bush and around a shed, I found myself in a garden. I wasn't sure if it belonged to our bungalow or the cottage next door, so I crept under the window just in case. Jumping a few feet over some rocks, I was on the beach. My footsteps crunched over pebbles as I ran to the water's edge.

The sea stretched out forever and the sky looked soft and clear above it. I found a flat pebble and skimmed it over the waves. It skipped three times then disappeared into a tangle of seaweed. I searched but couldn't see the seal. I should have brought the binoculars with me.

Two arms of rock curved round the beach like the front legs of a crab. It felt hidden away, secret; almost like it was waiting for someone or something. I took my earphones out. The waves whispered. *Shhh … shhhh.*

I was going into a sort of trance when a dark bird with white wing flashes streaked across my vision. I shielded my eyes and followed its flight. It had a rough cry something like *Gek-Gek*.

"The pirate of the seas!" someone shouted.

Startled, I turned. A figure was crouched, very still, on a flat rock. The person stood up, revealing a girl about my age. She nodded at the bird flying across the horizon.

"It kills and eats smaller birds, puffins even. It's called a Bonxie, or Great Skua to you."

She had a funny way of talking; kind of sing-song. As she spoke, she came closer, leaping from boulder to boulder like a goat. When a few feet away she said, "I'm Izzie Christie. You must be Jack."

Up close, she was skinny, with masses of crinkled brown hair. Her eyes weren't blue or grey, more ... silver. She frowned and squinted when she spoke.

"I live next door. My mum cleans for Maudie Moody when she lets the cottage out."

I was struggling to find something to say.

"That's the woman who owns Oz Cottage ... the bungalow you're in. She goes off to Australia for six months every year." She waited for me to answer.

"Ah," I managed. It wasn't a brilliant beginning and she looked bored already.

"Gotta get going," she said. 'See you round." She leapt easily over the rocks and up into the garden I'd just come through.

I decided to wait a few minutes to let her get inside her house before I sneaked past their window again. I skimmed another pebble across the water. This time it skipped four times.

Back in my room, I unzipped my guitar case and sat on the bed. I balanced my guitar on my knee and began strumming. Okay, it was only *Twinkle, Twinkle, Little Star*, but every rock star has to start somewhere. Mum banged on the wall between our rooms and called. "Not now, hon, please?"

I tried to strum quietly, but that didn't work. I needed sound to block out the thoughts I didn't want to think. The deafening silence made me uneasy and the tight feeling in my chest was creeping back. I untangled my iPod and climbed under the duvet to listen to some music

I woke up at some point and heard Mum crying. I shoved my earphones in deeper and turned the music up really loud.

"Lerwick, on the Shetland Islands, is Britain's most northerly town." We were parked near the quayside and Mum was reading from the tourist book. *"Situated on a natural harbour, the town is always buzzing with cruise ships, fishing vessels and yachts from around the world."* We both looked toward the boats. "It's busy all right," she said.

The seafront smelt of fish and salt. Gulls squatted on the decks of fishing boats picking at bits of the catch. Red, blue and yellow painted hulls bobbed on the water.

"The High Street in Lerwick has no shops; it is a small lane that runs between two rows of houses. The main shops are in stone-flagged Commercial Street. See page eleven."

She frowned. "It says here that the Shetland islanders have Viking blood … that their ancestors came from Scandinavia so they see themselves as more Norse than Scottish. The Vikings were a fierce race, weren't they?" She looked nervously in the rear-view mirror, as if she expected a horde of blond giants wearing winged helmets to attack the car at any moment.

"I think we're safe enough, Mum. They stopped pillaging a while back." She tutted and started the engine.

We found most of what Mum wanted in the main shopping centre, then bought a fish supper to eat back at the bungalow.

At three in the morning my room was *still* light. I couldn't sleep. The curtains were too thin and a weird pink light sneaked through and lit up the room.

"Doesn't it *ever* get dark around here?" I shouted at the cross-eyed koala. The quiet was a real problem too. I was used to the hum of cars throughout the night. I liked the traffic noise and living in a city. It made me feel part of the world, where things were happening.

I bet nothing ever happens here, I thought.

I slipped out of bed and helped myself to a yoghurt from the fridge. The floor tiles were cold beneath my feet so I went into the carpeted lounge. Smaller than the kitchen, it had one huge black leather sofa and a sort of bamboo coffee table. There was a picture of a great big red rock, presumably somewhere in Australia. Parrots hung on another wall next to a huge pipe that Mum said was a Didgeridoo; a type of musical instrument. The telly sat on another bamboo table in the corner. No satellite box I noticed and no DVD player either. The only decent piece of technology was mum's printer sitting in the corner blinking a steady green light like a lonely beacon. This room smelled like polish. The window faced away from the sea and up on the hill a circle of great stones huddled together like a group of old men whispering secrets. Everything about this place was creepy … alien. I didn't want to be here. I wanted to go back to Edinburgh.

I finished my yoghurt and licked the lid clean. On my way back to bed I noticed how the pink light flashed on the sink and taps in the kitchen and made strange reflections on the walls. I got that creepy feeling again. Throwing the empty yoghurt pot into the bin I caught sight of a slight movement to the side of the fridge.

Mice, I thought. *That'll really freak Mum out.*

The next morning, mum checked off her equipment before piling it into her backpack.

"Tripod, camera, cable release." She took another quick bite of toast. "It's the Northern Lights I really want to shoot, but I think we're maybe too late. They happen mostly in the winter." She made a 'tutting' noise with her tongue. "Oh come on, Jack. Crisps for breakfast is a ridiculously bad idea."

I opened the packet and switched on the telly. "What're the Northern Lights?"

"They're amazing, almost like a firework display but it's a natural phenomenon. You have to be in the north to see them; something to do with the weather conditions. They're bright colours, reds and greens, that fill the sky. If I get some good shots that new magazine said they'd take the lot."

"Slide film, macro lens." She tucked more bits into various pockets of her bag. "That should do it."

I noticed how thin she looked; her eyes seemed too big for her face and there were dark circles under them. A year ago one, of the older boys at school had shouted at me, "Hey, McKenzie! Your Mum's well fit!" At the time I didn't know whether to be pleased or angry; now I'd be pleased.

Wind rattled the window. "I'm staying here," I said.

"Don't you fancy an expedition? There's a rare plant on Shetland somewhere called the Mouse Ear." She laughed, "I'm going to try to find it and get some pictures." She hesitated. "Oh, go on ... come with me, Jack."

"No. I'm fine."

"Well, if you go down on the beach don't forget ..."

"My mobile," I finished for her.

"And?"

"Call you every two hours."

Mum tucked her black hair behind her ears and zipped up her red fleece. Tossing the backpack over her shoulder, she said:

"I'll be back by midday. The people next door left a note to say if we need anything so ..."

"Yeah, yeah."

"There's plenty of food in the fridge so ..."

"Go," I said.

I lay on the sofa with my earphones in and the sound down on the telly. I reckoned by the time I got back home my mates would be well ahead of me on computer games. I was wasting good gaming time being here.

A shadow fell across the room and I looked up to see a face pressed against the window. I leapt up from the sofa. It was the girl, Izzie … from next door. She made signs for me to open the door.

"I rang the bell twice," she said when I let her in. She looked accusingly at my iPod. "Do you live with that thing stuck in your ears?"

"What's it to you?" I said, annoyed.

"Oh, so you do speak," she said. "Come on."

"Where?"

"Out. You'll need a jacket."

"It's not raining," I said.

"It will," she replied.

I grabbed my hoodie and just remembered the house key before running after her, slamming the door behind me. She moved quickly over the hill in a kind of easy walk-run. I stumbled after her, trying to keep up. There was a sweetish smell of grass and sheep everywhere, who skittered out of our path, bleating. They weren't all white; some were black and some brown. Izzie didn't seem to notice. She had her hands shoved deep in her pockets and marched in front of me, head down, without speaking.

Eventually, she said, "There's something you should see, City Boy."

I caught her up and grabbed her shoulder to stop her. "What's this 'City Boy' stuff about? You called around for me. If you don't want me here …" I turned and stomped off in the opposite direction.

"Hey, wait," she called. "You're right, sorry. I was just teasing."

I took my time walking back to her.

"Anyway," she grinned, "you'd soon get lost wandering that way."

We'd been heading away from the house and now we zig-zagged down a rough track to the cliffs again.

"I want you to meet Tammie Norie ... the puffin," Izzie shouted above the noise. We'd reached the edge of the cliff where the grass was springy and damp with seawater. The screech of thousands of seabirds was deafening.

She dropped to her hands and knees and crawled towards a group of rocks. "Puffins are so tame we can get really close".

They were the weirdest things; like little penguins but with orange beaks, clown eyes and red feet. We were close enough to stretch out and touch one but they didn't seem at all bothered. They walked like clowns, too, because of their short legs. One crash-landed on the grass right beside me, making us laugh. Above the squawking, I heard a chainsaw.

"What's *that?*"

Izzie shouted, "It's a puffin growling."

"No *way!*"

"Yes, way."

I heard it again and laughed until I cried. The little birds' growling *was* hysterical. Izzie laughed too. She pointed out other birds to me: fulmars, oystercatchers with orange spindle beaks, and scories, like swooping gulls. This girl knew a lot about birds ... and it was interesting stuff.

It rained but I hardly noticed. It stopped and the sun came out again. I don't know how long we would have stayed there, lying on our stomachs, enjoying the circus antics of the birds, but a double shadow fell over us.

"Um … excuse me," a voice said. A tall man and a short woman looked down on us. They both wore black capes and carried long, knobbly walking sticks. He spoke with a Welsh accent.

Izzie and I stood up, dusting the grass from our knees.

"We understand that there's a certain type of frog hereabouts that was used as an ancient charm and has mystical powers." The man leaned forward and almost whispered. "You … ah … couldn't tell us where we might find some of these frogs, could you?"

"You mean the Bumpy Rocket Frog, or *Litoria inermis,* to give it its proper name?" Izzie asked.

"We do?"

Izzie nodded. She looked very serious. "You need to head for Eldritch Craig. It's a standing stone over that way."

"Eldritch?"

"Craig," Izzie said. "It means ghostly stone. Devil's stone."

The tall man looked down at the small woman and she looked up at him, her face all smiles.

"You'll need a good strong bramble branch," Izzie added.

The man raised thick white eyebrows.

"To beat the bushes with. It has to be bramble … but I expect you know that already," Izzie continued.

I was beginning to wonder if Izzie was as serious as she sounded.

The man tried to look as if he knew what she was talking about. "Oh, of course, the bramble stick." He took a crumpled notebook and a pencil from an inside pocket, slowly unwound a rubber band, and licked the point of the pencil. "What time of day would you suggest we look for the ... um ... the Bumpy Rocket Frog?"

"Turn of the moon's your best bet," said Izzie.

The man mumbled "Moon" and jotted it in the book.

Izzie glanced across at me and I saw mischief in her eyes.

The woman tugged at the man's sleeve and stood on tiptoe to whisper something in his ear.

"Ah, good point, my love, good point," the man said. "My wife wishes to know how we'll be able to tell the ... the ... um ... Bumpy Rocket Frog from any ordinary frog?"

"It goes *crick,"* I said. The three of them turned to me.

"Crick?"

"Instead of croak."

The man scribbled madly in his notebook again, then folded it neatly, wound the rubber band around it twice and put it back in his inside pocket.

"Thank you both *so* much."

We watched as they walked up the hill in the direction Izzie had pointed. The man's long loping strides and the woman's teetering tiptoe walk, trying to keep up. Their cloaks swirled out behind them in the breeze.

"You made that up, didn't you!" I said.

Izzie snorted with laughter. "Not the bit about there being a Bumpy Rocket Frog. That's true enough. And I pointed them in the right direction too … it comes from Australia. But the other stuff?" She shrugged. "Let's call it creative thinking."

"You're crazy," I said laughing too.

"Well then, so are you."

She got down in a frog crouch and started shouting "Crick! Crick! Crick!" I joined her and we shouted and bounced along until we were both rocking with hysteria.

I stopped suddenly. I hadn't laughed like this since … since the thing happened. I shouldn't be laughing.

I remembered my promise to Mum and patted my back pocket for my mobile. It wasn't there.

"I left my phone behind," I said. "I'm supposed to phone my mum." I was annoyed at myself. I knew mum would make a fuss if I didn't call her.

"I'm going home for lunch anyway." Izzie dragged her wild hair into a thick column, tucked it into her collar and pulled her hood up.

We heard the distant roar of a motorbike. We were almost home when the rider zoomed past us on the cliff road below. I recognised him and his red and black boots and froze.

"He was on the ferry," I said to Izzie. "He's got his name tattooed on his arm under a dagger dripping blood. *Slasher!*" We both grinned. I decided not to mention the throwing up on his boots bit.

"Here for the Simmer dim Rally, I expect," Izzie replied. Slasher and his bike disappeared behind the hill. Izzie saw my blank expression. "It's a motorbike rally, held here every year." She made a face. "He's really early though; it isn't for another month yet ... not 'til June."

I called Mum. She hadn't found her Mouse Ear flower.

"It only grows on the two hills on the island of Unst, she said. "Do you know it was discovered in 1837 by someone who was the same age as you when he found it?"

"Fascinating. Kids obviously didn't have anything interesting to do in those days."

"What like computer games, you mean?"

"Exactly."

"I'll be about another hour," she said. "You okay?"

"Yeah. I'm at the house with Izzie, the girl from next door."

I heard the relief in her voice. "That's good. Jack. It's just ... I worry. You know why."

"Okay. See you later." I ended the conversation as quickly as I could, leaned over to put my phone on the worktop, but it slipped through my fingers, dropped with a crack onto the tiled kitchen floor and skidded out of view.

I got down and felt between the fridge and the kitchen unit. I couldn't find it so I got up, shoved the fridge to the left and got down on my hands and knees again.

And that's when I found myself nose-to-fang with a massive red tarantula.

2. Izzie-zoo

Eight red and brown hairy legs ambled out of the gap and crawled towards me.

"Omigod! Omigod!" I screamed. It was a big girly scream too. I backed away pushing Izzie with one trembling hand and pointing with the other. "Look! ... There! ... There!"

Catching sight of the giant spider, Izzie froze. She stood open-mouthed staring at it in a kind of trance with such a weird look on her face that I thought, *God, now she's gonna faint.*

"Get me something to kill it with!" *Kill it?* I must have been off my head. Like I was really going to tackle a poisonous tarantula.

It was Izzie's turn to push *me* away. "*Don't* touch it," she said. I was really scared and very relieved that she was going to deal with it. But what happened next frightened me more than the spider.

She deliberately placed her hand on the floor, *right in front of it*. It kept moving, slowly, up onto her fingers and into her palm; its thick hairy legs moving in a slow dance like a winding down robot.

"It'll bite you, you idiot!"

"Shut up," she hissed. "Quick, open the door."

I certainly wasn't going to argue with a girl holding a venomous spider so I unlocked the front door. Slowly, Izzie followed me, holding her arm straight out in front of her. She was *smiling*. The tarantula relaxed in her palm like a huge tomato stalk.

"Pull the bushes aside and help me get through my garden without disturbing her," Izzie said calmly.

"Her?" To my annoyance I could hear the tremble in my voice.

"She's a female. And what a beautiful girl you are too, aren't you, my sweet," Izzie blew kisses at the fat-bodied hairy thing on her hand.

What a weirdo, I thought. *She probably cuddles pythons too.*

I kept as far away as possible, while trying not to look like a complete wimp. Izzie walked carefully, putting one foot steadily before the other, making sure she didn't trip. We reached the door of the shed and she whispered, "Unlock the padlock. The key's under that stone."

I could see a large, round stone near the door and could also see there was writing on it but I wasn't going to take my eyes off the spider for anything. What if it jumped? What if it jumped on *me*?

"Come *on*," Izzie said.

I pushed at the stone with my foot until it was out of, what I guessed would be spider-jump range and picked up a key.

"Now open the door and put on the light," she said laughing. "Welcome to the Izzie-zoo."

Two wooden shelves held several tanks. I could see something moving in at least one of them and thought, *If this girls loved tarantulas, what else had she got in there?*

"It's okay. It's quite safe," Izzie said. "There's nothing in here that will grab you by the throat … yet. *Brachypelma smithi.* The Mexican Red-Kneed tarantula," she explained when she'd dropped the spider gently into a plastic tank. "They're harmless to humans. Their bite will hurt, but their venom is weaker than a bee's."

"Never mind the venom. I think I'd die of a heart attack if that thing bit me. If I'd known there were tarantulas wandering around the Shetland Islands I wouldn't have come."

"There aren't." Izzie turned to me with that odd intense look on her face. "It's far too cold. Tarantulas come from warm climates. This one has escaped from somewhere." She spoke affectionately to the spider. "You'll be safe now, little one."

I'll be safe now, was what I was thinking. My heartbeat gradually returned to normal and I was able to drag my eyes away from the hairy monster in the tank.

The shed was filled with the usual rubbish: old suitcases, paint pots, gardening tools and a cardboard box full of dusty light bulbs. Two broken tennis rackets and several golf clubs leaned into a corner. An earthy smell was coming from two other tanks and I moved closer.

"Meet Karma, my chameleon, and Bombina, my Oriental Fire-Bellied Toad."

"Cool," I said and meant it. I'd only seen creatures like these on telly. It really *was* cool that Izzie owned them.

She took a spray gun and spritzed water into the chameleon's tank.

"You giving it a shower?"

She laughed. "No, I have to keep the humidity

right. That's why I have that heat lamp too."

"How come you *know* all this stuff, about animals and birds and everything?"

"It's what I love. I want to be another Uhlenbrock."

I tapped the chameleon's tank. "What's an Uhlenbrock?"

"Don't do that!" Izzie flicked my arm. "It's not a 'what' it's a 'who.' Dr Charlotte Uhlenbrock. She's amazing."

"Oh, isn't she that fit woman who got jumped on by a gorilla?"

Izzie's silvery eyes narrowed. "She's that intelligent woman with a doctorate in zoology and a passion for wildlife ... yes."

"I'm gonna have my own band, be a rock star," I said.

Focused again on the tarantula, Izzie ignored me. "I wonder where you came from?" she said, then turned to me. "Come on. Let's get something to eat. And *don't* tell my mum and dad about the spider."

"Won't they notice it?"

"My dad can't get his wheelchair in here and luckily mum won't come anywhere near the shed since I got Karma. She was scared enough of my little toad. God knows what would happen if she found a tarantula."

Izzie's house was yellow inside ... *very* yellow: yellow curtains and yellow walls. Her parents sat either side of a huge table, even the tablecloth was yellow. Mr Christie looked like a great bear. I could see where Izzie got her crinkly hair from. His was darker though, with streaks of grey and he had a beard and bushy eyebrows. When he looked up at me and smiled, I saw where she got her odd silvery eyes from too. A fat Siamese cat snored on his lap.

"Welcome, lad," Mrs Christie said. She pulled out a chair and I sat down. "You'll stop for lunch? We've tattie soup and brunnies."

I had no idea what 'brunnies' were but the tattie soup sounded good. It was. Mrs Christie talked non-stop although Mr Christie didn't say much at all. He'd moved his wheelchair to the side of the table when the soup came, leaving the mountain of bits and pieces he'd been working on when we came in. It was an odd mix of things: putty, light bulbs, three or four miniature boats and a set of scary-looking, long metal tools, hooks and knives, laid out in a line like a surgeon's tray.

Izzie saw me looking. "Dad makes boats in bulbs," she said. "They're beautiful."

Mr Christie gave his daughter an affectionate smile. The pain in my chest was there in a flash and I swallowed hard. I looked at the cat, still lying on his lap. It stretched, yawned and went back to sleep.

The "brunnies" were a bit like flapjacks and we had them with syrup. Mr Christie immediately went back to his boats in bulbs and Izzie stood behind him with her hand on his shoulder giving me a running commentary. Mrs Christie talked, mostly to herself, as she rattled soup bowls in the sink.

"First, there's the tinted putty. Dad tools and paints it to look like the sea. It takes six to eight weeks to dry." Izzie pointed to several coloured pieces on the table.

I was still thinking about the tarantula. *Where did it come from? A gigantic poisonous spider was not the sort of thing you lose, like an umbrella.*

"Jack?" Izzie called my attention back to Mr Christie's boats. "Then he builds the galleys. They're Viking boats, with masts that collapse. They fold along the deck. When he's put the galley through the end of the light bulb, he raises the mast by pulling on these threads."

Mr Christie showed me, his huge hands tugging at the threads.

"I saw Lily Fagan in Commercial Road today. Her twins have got nits." Mrs Christie said to no one in particular.

It was all so calm and friendly in their house and I kept thinking: *They don't know there's a venomous spider lurking in their garden shed.*

The Siamese cat leapt onto the table and batted at a piece of putty.

"Minx, get down," Mrs Christie said. The cat flicked the putty off the table and peered over to see where it landed.

Mrs Christie scooped the cat into her arms and gave it a quick kiss on the head before dropping it back onto Mr Christie's lap. "Your mother popped in first thing this morning," she said. "Just to say would we keep an eye on you, like?"

I gritted my teeth. Well that explained why Izzie was in a bad mood when she came around to call for me this morning. She'd been told to "keep an eye on me." *Thanks for that, Mum,* I thought.

"Your Mum's a pretty wee thing. Where does she come from?"

"Edinburgh," I said, "but her parents are from the Philippines. Manila."

"Ahh, so that's where she gets her beautiful dark hair and eyes. You're like her, lad."

I nodded. I was used to being told how much I looked like Mum. A small panic tightened my chest under my ribs. I didn't want to talk about my family.

"Except your hair is curlier. Where ..."

Izzie saved me. She thrust my jacket at me. "Jack's going to help me clean out my zoo," she said, warning me with wide eyes not mention the tarantula.

Mrs Christie gave an exaggerated shudder. "Why any daughter of mine would want those horrible creatures is beyond me. Have you seen that lizard? Creepy thing."

"She loves them," Mr Christie said, without looking up.

"Aye, well." Mrs Christie re-arranged the tea towel over the cooker bar and changed the subject. "That wee tramp that's been around lately ... the one that looks like a good gust of wind would blow him over ... Lily Fagan says he lives on seaweed and cockles. No one's ever seen him buy food."

Mr Christie grunted and I saw he was laughing to himself.

But Izzie tensed. She seemed suddenly very interested in what her mother was saying. "Is that the guy living in the cave?" she said.

"Aye. Lily Fagan says he's that anti-social that if

he speaks it's like he's hurt his mouth. Mind, who knows what the poor man's been through in his life. He must have a reason to hide himself away from people like that."

"Umm. Come on." Izzie grabbed my arm.

"There was a witch lived in that cave when I was girl," Mrs Christie was saying. "For the price of a couple of mackerel she'd charm your warts."

After the warmth and comfort of the yellow kitchen the shed was cold and smelt damp. We checked the tarantula; she seemed to be sleeping although I couldn't see much difference from when she was awake.

"I've had a thought," Izzie said.

I resisted the urge to make some sarcastic comment like I would to my mates. Somehow I knew Izzie wouldn't let me get away with it.

"About Octavia."

"Who?"

"The tarantula. I've named her Octavia."

"Oh *have* you? Let me remind you whose house it was in, and who found it in the first place."

"You want her? Here, she's yours," Izzie lifted the lid of the tank and dipped her fingers in."

"No! No!" I backed away.

"Fine, that's settled then," she said lowering the lid again.

I knew I'd been bettered and I didn't like it. "You haven't got any food for it, anyway." I said sulking. I took the broken tennis racket and played air guitar.

"I've got the mealie worms I feed to Karma and Bombina," she said. "That'll do until I can trap some crickets."

"Crickets?"

"Tarantulas don't eat food like we do. They catch insects and inject them with venom. That paralyzes the prey. When the venom breaks down the insect's body tissue, the tarantula can suck the liquid up." She made a slurping noise.

"*Nice*," I said playing a C on the tennis racket.

"That plastic tank's too small for her. Help me line this one with some moss."

We were so busy getting the new tank ready that we didn't see Minx creep into the shed. But Minx saw the spider.

The crash made us both turn sharply … too late. The upturned tank was already on the floor, the tarantula crawling out.

"No!" Izzie shouted in horror as the cat flicked a paw towards the spider. Minx batted at the tarantula three more times before howling with pain as the spider's fangs sunk into his paw.

"Get away!" Izzie shouted and I didn't know if she meant the cat or me. I didn't need telling anyway. I'd backed myself into a corner of the shed, behind an old filing cabinet. Minx shook his paw violently, which sent the tarantula wheeling across the shed floor. The cat sprinted out the door like his tail was on fire.

"I'll get Minx." I said. The Siamese was hiding beneath a bush making weird hissing and growling sounds and licking his paw.

"It's okay … it's okay" I whispered. He calmed

down enough to let me pick him up and I carried him back to Izzie.

At the door of the shed I called, "All clear?"

"All clear," she said.

She'd got the tarantula back into the tank but it wasn't moving much. Izzie was shaking. "I should have closed the door," she said. "It's my fault. I always close the door."

She took the cat from me and cradled him in her arms. "Poor Minx, I'm sorry, I'm sorry."

"Will he die?" I whispered.

"No, I don't think so, but we'd better get him to the vet right away. Sheila Voss lives in that croft just along the road."

I followed Izzie out of the gate as mum pulled up in the Clio. She wound down the window. "What's up?"

"Izzie's cat ... um, this is Izzie ..." Mum and Izzie exchanged smiles. "Her cat got um ... hurt," I said.

"Can I help?"

"No, the vet lives right there, thanks," Izzie said.

"I'll be back in a minute, Mum."

Sheila Voss's croft, as Izzie called it, was just a few yards further down the lane. It was built on the slope of a hill and was small and old and white. A brass plate beside the door said: Sheila Voss RCVS.

Izzie was about to press the bell when we heard voices from inside, angry voices. She hesitated.

A woman said, "You fool. Thanks to your stupidity

we lost almost half the consignment."

A man with an English accent shouted back. "I wanted *one*, that's all, just *one*. I've always wanted one. If you'd let me ..."

Minx yowled again and licked his paw. Izzie pressed the doorbell. Instantly, the argument stopped. A woman's voice called, "Who is it?"

"It's me. Izzie. There's something wrong with Minx."

There was a scuffle and whispering from inside and eventually the door opened. A small woman with short reddish hair and dangling earrings said, "Come in, Izzie. What's wrong? Here, bring Minx into the surgery."

"I think something bit him," Izzie avoided looking the vet in the eye.

Sheila Voss gently shaved of a patch of fur on Minx's paw. "It's a bite all right, but it doesn't look like a rat did it. She gave Izzie an odd look. "You didn't see what bit him, did you? It looks almost like ..."

"Stop making such a fuss, you spoiled baby," Izzie interrupted, talking to the cat. She rubbed his ears.

I was waiting just outside the open door of the surgery and heard the click of a door. Someone let himself out and slunk past the window with his head down and his hood up.

Sheila Voss washed the cat's paw, put antiseptic cream on and gave him an antibiotic injection. He howled more at that than he had done at the tarantula bite.

"That should do it," she said to Izzie. "But bring

him back tomorrow and I'll give him a quick once over."

"I will," Izzie said. "Thanks."

"You should have told her." We were walking back to the bungalow. "You should have told her about the tarantula."

"No." Izzie said. "Minx will be fine. If everyone knows about Octavia she'll be taken away from me. People are scared of spiders, especially ones as big as she is. They don't understand them. They'll want to kill her."

"She's not yours anyway. Someone must have lost her."

"I've been thinking about that. You'd think if someone lost their pet there'd be something on the local news warning people about a missing tarantula. Or posters on lamp-posts or … something." She opened her gate and dropped Minx gently into her garden. The Siamese trotted away, the spider bite already forgotten. "It was what I was going to tell you before Minx got into the shed. I think I might know where Octavia came from," Izzie said.

We pushed past the bush and came out by the front door of the bungalow.

"I think it's to do with smugglers and I bet the Eigg man is the mastermind."

While I looked at her as if she'd just fallen off a Martian spaceship, Izzie whispered, "Don't tell your mum about Octavia. See you tomorrow."

Egg men and smugglers? She must be nuts, I thought.

3. Clickimin Broch

"Do you have to put ketchup on it, Jack?"

"Yes." Mum had made this great Filipino dish called pork and chicken adobo. "So the cat is okay?"

"Yeah."

"And you don't know *what* bit it?"

"No." I avoided looking at her. We were in the lounge, eating off trays and watching telly.

"Pity about your mobile. We'll take it back to the shop when we get home. Maybe they can fix it."

"Mmm. I just dropped it ... can't get a signal or anything now. Can I have the salt, please?"

Mum talked about her day's work. "This place is a photographer's heaven. The seascapes are magical. There're islands dotted all over the seas and dramatic rocks and cliffs. And there's this wonderful clear light here too. I don't think I could capture half of what I'd like to if I stayed for a hundred years."

She looked happy, happier than she'd been for a long time. Her eyes sparkled. "And everyone's so friendly."

I told her about the puffins and their chain-saw growl and the Izzie-zoo, but *not* about the tarantula. It was hard not to tell her about that. Thinking about it, it was pretty cool and I wasn't really *that* scared. In fact, if I hadn't been there I don't know what Izzie would have done. Pity, my mobile was broken. I thought of several mates I could have texted.

Hi how R u? I
found a tarantula
2day btw - itz
pritE kewl I think
I mite kEp it.

I was daydreaming about the replies I'd get, when Mum ruined everything.

"While we're here, we need to talk about your father, Jack. You just can't go on pretending nothing happened."

I felt the familiar pain. The pain came on every time Dad was mentioned. "Yes, I can." I got up, leaving my tray on the floor and went to my room.

Mum followed me. "Jack, please don't do this."

I grabbed my iPod and switched it on full blast.

Mum tugged at the wires and the earphones dropped out of my ears.

"I'll be sitting outside with a glass of wine, Jack. I'll be there for a while if you want to come and talk to me."

I plugged the earphones right back in and played my music for hours. I lay on my bed with my eyes closed and sang along as loudly as I could, only stopping when my throat hurt so much I couldn't sing any more.

It was *still* light but grey and rainy. I heard Mum in the room next door, getting ready for bed. She must have given up waiting for me. I hated her for trying to make me talk and I hated myself for shutting her out. She didn't deserve it. But most of all I hated Dad for what had happened to us.

I got my pyjama bottoms on and slipped under the duvet. Before I lay down I looked out over the beach. It was raining and the strange light on the wet rocks made them shine like mirrors. Just past Izzie's house I could see the flicker of a fire. *Bit wet for a barbecue,* I thought. As I peered closer I saw a dark figure huddled over the flames. As I watched he stood, stretched and arranged his coat over his head before squatting down beside the fire again. I tried the binoculars to get a better look but the rain against the window pane made it impossible to see. I gave up.

The hammering on my window startled me awake. Izzie's face, framed by her mess of frizzy hair peered in at me, "Come on!" she mouthed.

"What? Who?" I rubbed my eyes.

"Get up!" She beckoned frantically.

I lay back down and pulled the duvet over my head. "Go away."

The window rattled again. "Come on, Jack."

Mum knocked at the bedroom door, "Jack? What is it? Can I come in?"

I made a loud huffy noise. "Can't anyone get any sleep around here?"

Mum walked in anyway, saw Izzie outside, waved and opened the window. "Morning, Izzie, I didn't introduce myself properly yesterday. I'm Marissa."

The cold air streamed into the room.

"Hello," Izzie smiled.

"Can you two get to know each other someplace else and shut that window?" I grunted. They seemed to find that very amusing.

"Come on in," Mum beckoned. "I'm making pancakes."

"Cool." Izzie disappeared and Mum left my room. I heard her let Izzie in at the front door. I could hear them talking together when I went into the bathroom for a shower.

The pancakes with Maple syrup were good and it was now warm and sunny outside. Monday was starting well. Mum couldn't wait to get out with her camera.

"If you two don't mind, I'll get going while this gorgeous light is still here. It changes so quickly. See you later." She grabbed up her camera bag.

In Izzie's shed, I took her word for it when she told me the spider was fine after its fight with Minx. It's not easy to tell what a tarantula is feeling. It just squatted there looking hairy and scary. Izzie had tidied the tank and put a jam jar lid of water in.

"I'll just check out Karma the Chameleon and Bombina your Oriental Fire-Bellied Toad." I'd made a point of remembering their names and what they were, and it got me a look of approval.

"Give them a spray, would you?"

Karma was awesome, about a third of a metre long with a flat head, but I really liked little Bombina. His back was bright green and black, he jumped around all over the place and you could see his belly was brilliant orange and black. Sometimes he made squeaky noises as well and he swam in his own little swimming pool. I watched, fascinated, and then lifted the lid off his tank.

"Don't mess around with Bombina too much," Izzie warned. "He's toxic." I pulled my hand out in a flash. She laughed. "He probably won't hurt you unless you've got cuts on your hand or something."

"What was that weird stuff you said about smugglers and an egg man yesterday?"

Izzie put the lid on Octavia's tank and screwed it down. "I need your help to spy on him."

"Who?"

"The Eigg man."

"Why do you call him that? Does he keep chickens?" I asked.

She laughed. "No, E-I-G-G. It's a small island in the Inner Hebrides. Someone said that's where he comes from. He's the tramp who lives in the cave … the one my mum was talking about yesterday."

"Why on earth would you want to spy on a tramp?"

I sprayed Karma and he looked like he was enjoying it. He closed his big buggy eyes and swayed from side to side. I got a chance to see his feet up close. There were five neat toes on each foot; the back feet had three toes outside and two inside. The front feet were the opposite way around. *I bet Izzie could tell me exactly why,* I thought.

Izzie checked the digital thermometer hanging on the wall. We'd made sure the shed door *was* shut so that there was no chance of Minx creeping in again.

"Because I'm sure he's got something to do with the wildlife smuggling that goes on here," Izzie continued.

I was stunned for a minute. "I've never heard of smuggling wildlife."

"It's a big thing. My Uncle Duncan is a policeman and did a talk at our school all about it. All sorts of animals and plants are brought into the country illegally and some come through Lerwick."

"And you think that spider … I mean Octavia … might have been smuggled in?"

"It makes sense," she said. "Tarantulas and scorpions were some of the creatures that Uncle Duncan mentioned. Gorillas, I remember, as well."

I scanned the shed uneasily. "You've haven't got any gorillas tucked away in here, have you?"

Izzie laughed. "No, don't panic."

Her zoo duties taken care of, Izzie waved me outside and padlocked the shed door. When she tucked the key under smooth stone I bent down to read the words painted on it. It said, *"Turn me over"* so, of course, I turned it over and on the other side it said, *"Ah, that's better."*

"Oh, ha ha," I said, peeved at being caught out.

Izzie was laughing again. "Just one of Dad's jokes," she said.

"Don't you think it's a dumb idea to hide a key *under* a stone and then trick people into moving the stone?"

"Nobody here is going to break into the shed. I lock it to keep my creatures in, not people out. You're not in the big, bad, city now, you know."

"At least we don't get smugglers," I argued.

"No, just murderers and …" She stopped. "This is pointless. Look, come to Sheila Voss's with me to check that Minx is okay and I'll tell you my plan about the Eigg man." She picked up the fat Siamese who was wailing and twisting itself around her legs.

We sat in the waiting room while Sheila clipped a dog's claws; it howled as if she was clipping his feet, and then she rubbed cream onto a hamster that was going bald. Yuk. Minx remembered what had happened to him the last time he was brought in and squirmed and yowled as only Siamese cats could.

"Minx is fine, the bite's healing nicely. Just keep up the antiseptic cream for the rest of the week" Sheila said.

"I pretty much knew that this morning when he stole Dad's kipper off the plate," Izzie said. "Can I show Jack the ponies?"

"You can do more than that. You can help me with the mucking out," Sheila said. "I've got a dog with a boil and a parrot that flew into a ceiling fan to see … then I'll meet you in the field."

Mucking out? That didn't sound like fun to me and, as it turned out, I was right. First, we dropped Minx into Izzie's garden, then hurried back to Sheila's house. As we reached the gate into the field, a dog started barking like crazy; it sounded like a *big* dog and I stopped in my tracks.

Izzie saw me. "Don't worry. That's just Louis's Rottweiler. King. He's chained up outside that caravan. He can't hurt you. What do you think of that?" Izzie pointed proudly at a white van with cartoons of Shetland ponies painted on it.

"Cool."

Izzie grinned. "Dad painted them. Sheila thought it might advertise the Shetland ponies and help get some funds to help her look after them. She doesn't drive it much though. She cycles most places."

Sheila had twelve Shetland ponies; all short, fat and hairy. As soon as we appeared at the gate they trotted over, whinnying a welcome. They were cute I have to say; muddy, but cute.

We leaned over the gate and the ponies crowded round pushing and shoving each other to get close. Sheila had given us mints to feed them with. Izzie knew all their names and told me some. "That's Kilty, Conner and Amber … just look at her lovely eyes. The little black one with his mane over one eye is Crumble and this pest here," she stretched her hand through the bars and petted a light tan pony with a white saddle shape on his back, "is called Nuggle because he was always trying to charge off into the sea. Sheila named him after a local legend; a Nuggle is a pony that's really a kelpie … a water sprite."

Sheila came out of the croft to join us. She'd changed into old clothes and carried rubber boots and gloves but still wore her dangling earrings. "If any one tried to ride the Nuggle it would gallop off to the nearest water and drown the rider," she said in a pretend scary voice.

"Nice," I backed away.

The ponies were fun, crunching mints with their rubbery lips raised over their teeth. I patted one. His coat was thick but soft.

"They're getting their summer coats now. Their fur is much coarser in winter, because they need all the warmth they can get," Izzie said.

"Here you go. This should do the job." Sheila handed us each a pair of boots and a pair of gloves.

Izzie's fitted her but my boots were too tight and the gloves were dropping off my hands.

"Gosh, you've got big feet," Izzie said when I complained. "Those boots are gi-normous."

There were two sheds, or field shelters, as Sheila called them. "Right," she said, "Izzie knows the score. First, we take out the feed tubs and water buckets."

Inside stank of poo and pee. Several flies buzzed. "Gross," I said taking several steps back. Izzie and Sheila laughed.

"Here's the wheelbarrow. You two can make a start," Sheila said.

Izzie handed me a pitchfork, "If you fork the manure and wet bedding into the wheelbarrow, I'll use the shovel."

"Thanks," I said flatly.

Sheila went for the fresh straw. "How often does she have to do this?" I said, screwing up my nose against the stink. The wet straw was heavy and smelly.

"Every day." Izzie shovelled a pile of manure into the barrow. "I help when I can. People bring ponies to her when they can't look after them any more. Sometimes they're ill. She does all this on her own, you know. It's loads of work and costs loads of money too. She really loves them. They're her life."

Several of the Shetlands lined up watching us, huge eyes following every move. Occasionally, they'd flick their tails or toss their manes or take a nip at each other. The one called Nuggle sneaked into the stall when I wasn't looking and nudged me from behind. I fell face first into the wet straw. Izzie laughed so much she cried.

I looked down at my brand new T-shirt and I could have cried too. It was smeared with something disgusting.

"Sorry about your trendy clothes, City Boy," she said.

"You're just jealous you … you … Island Girl."

"Island Girl? Island Girl? Is that your best insult?" Izzie hooted.

When we'd filled the wheelbarrow, Sheila showed me where to dump the muck on the manure pile. The boots hurt my feet and I kind of hobbled with the wheelbarrow, which made them laugh all over again. Sheila brought a bale of clean straw. We forked it over the floor, fluffing it up and evening it out. I was pretty good at that. The flies disappeared and the shelters smelled clean and fresh like summertime.

"I think all that work deserves a good lunch," Sheila said. I realized I was starving. We patted and petted the ponies and they crowded in on us, happy to take all the fuss we could give them. Although Nuggle was the smallest he kicked out at the others if they came too close to us.

We heard a motorbike screech to a halt and I saw Sheila shield her eyes and look towards her house. "Won't be a minute," she said.

I followed her gaze, and there sitting in the driveway, astride his huge black and silver machine was someone I recognised.

"It's Slasher," I whispered to Izzie and ducked down behind the ponies.

"What are you doing?"

"Hiding."

"Why?"

Reluctantly, I told Izzie what had happened on the ferry.

"So you chucked up all over his boots?" She was laughing at me again.

"Shut up! He'll hear you."

"Oh, *excellent*."

"He didn't think so. Will you *shut up*."

This only made her cackle even more and Sheila and Slasher turned to look. I quickly ducked into the field shelter and peered out over the bottom half of the door to watch them.

When they'd finished talking, Sheila shook her head. I saw Slasher kick start the bike into action and heard the roar as he took off up the road. Sheila shrugged and called to us. "I'm finished now, Anyone for sausage rolls?"

We were smelly and muddy and Sheila made us scrub our hands with medicated soap before we ate. Izzie must have told her about me being sick on Slasher because I could hear them giggling in the kitchen. When she'd cleaned up, Sheila brought Cokes and a plate of warm sausage rolls to us on the patio overlooking the beach. The Rottweiler started barking again, deep loud barks but Sheila shouted, "King!" and it stopped right away.

"Louis is still renting your caravan then?" Izzie said.

"Yes, until he can afford a place of his own."

They were talking about people I didn't know so I took another sausage roll and leaned back in the comfortable garden chair. I found a blister between my thumb and finger. I'd never had a blister before. The sea was still new to me; the rhythm, the swish, swish and the changing colours were fascinating. We were so close to the water I could smell the iron scent of the seaweed. I breathed in deeply. I felt good.

Sheila was telling Izzie, "They have to have passports now, you know, just like people. And every new pony I get sees the farrier, the equine dentist and gets treated for worms."

I tried not to think about the worms while I was eating my sausage roll.

"That lot costs about a hundred pounds per pony, without feed and hay. On top of that, there's the field rent, fencing costs … the list goes on and on."

I helped myself to the last sausage roll when they weren't looking.

"I don't know how you manage," Izzie said.

"I manage; I'll do whatever I have to do to keep my ponies." There was an angry edge to her voice.

Izzie went to take a sausage roll, saw I'd eaten the last one and gave me a dirty look. I shrugged and grinned. She turned back to Sheila, "What about the book you wrote? Is that selling?"

Sheila smiled. "Frank at the pet shop in town has shifted a few copies for me, but it hasn't made the bestseller list yet." She fluffed up the back of her red hair and struck a pose. "Pity, I had my photo taken specially for the cover."

They were quiet for a minute and I took the chance to ask Sheila what Slasher wanted.

She looked puzzled. "Slasher? The biker you mean? The one you ...?"

"Yeah, yeah, okay." I didn't want them to start giggling about me being sick on Slasher's boot again.

"I don't know. It was odd really. He said he wanted to be sure that I was the vet and that I lived here ... just in case. I said I was and I did, and he said thanks and goodbye."

"I stink. I need a shower." I said when we left Sheila's.

"Me too, meet you afterwards. I'll tell you about the Eigg man."

"Isn't that a song?"

"What?"

"I am the egg man, coo-coo-ca-choo."

Izzie squinted her silver eyes at me as if *I* was nuts.

Wet hair didn't suit Izzie: it was flat and straight and stuck to her head, but she certainly looked cleaner and smelled better after her shower. So did I. We took off up the hill towards the group of stones I'd seen on the night we arrived. They were further away and much bigger than I'd realized. When we got there I saw most of them were taller than me.

"We get people up here worshipping in mid-summer," Izzie said. "Sometimes they throw flowers and tie bows and things around the stones."

"Why?"

"Dunno. The stones aren't what I wanted to show you. We need to go a bit further. Run!" she said and we did, wildly; shouting as we bounced over the springy grass, yelling as we leapt over small rocks and trickling streams. Apart from the sheep and ponies, the wind was the only sound high up on the moor. It tugged at my hair and made my eyes water.

"Beat you to that big boulder," Izzie said pointing, as she took off like a racehorse. I sprinted after her but she was faster.

She was almost at the stone when I shouted, "I can't run anymore, I've got a stitch." I bent over clutching my side.

Izzie trotted back to me but as soon as she got level, I raced off towards the boulder and got there first, whooping in triumph.

"Cheat, cheat, never beat, City Boy," she called.

We were both whacked and walked the rest of the way. The weather had changed again and the air was cold and clammy. I pulled my hoodie up around my neck. We reached a pathway, lined on each side with grass and a fence of wooden poles. It led to a round stone building with a low wall around it. From a distance it looked like a huge hat.

"This is it. It's Clikimin Broch. It's a kind of tower but the top half has disappeared over the last few hundred years," Izzie said. "Come and see."

Even though there was a road across the top of the hills and another leading past the loch, there was no one else around. We had the whole place to ourselves. The wind made a noise like a faraway train and rippled the grass on the hill in waves. I'd got so used to the sound of sheep and ponies I hardly noticed the bleating or neighing any more. We stopped talking just to listen to the silence.

Then we ran again. In and out of the tunnels and pathways, leaping onto the walls, across the arches and around the broch. We ran for the sheer hell of it; up and down the steps, in and around and through and out again.

Eventually, I collapsed onto the ground inside and leaned back against the flat stone wall gasping for breath.

Izzie joined me. "Isn't this the greatest place?" She was bent over, her hands on her knees gulping in air.

"It's like the best den … *anywhere.*"

She was obviously pleased I was impressed and hunched down beside me.

"I bet it's really creepy at night though." I was still panting

"It is. You'd better watch out for the *trows* with that guitar playing of yours." Izzie wiggled her hands and made a pretend scared face.

"What are *trows?*"

"Nasty wee things; they're small, dark creatures that come out at night, they *looooove* musicians. They'll drag you down into the depths of their *trowie knowes* to play at their wedding feasts. You'll think only days have passed but in the real world it could be years."

I was quite chuffed that Izzie thought of me

a musician seeing as I hadn't quite mastered Twinkle, Twinkle yet.

"You were going to tell me about this Eigg man?"

"Aye, he's a phoney … a fake."

4. The Viking

Izzie elaborated. "Everyone here's seen the Eigg man striding on the moors or beachcombing. Long messy hair, tangled beard, ragged clothes … your stereotypical tramp."

"So?"

"Well. last week I was up here when he passed by. He didn't see me and there was no one else around. He was taking photos of the broch and walking as normally as you like. But as soon as some tourists turned up, he hid the camera in his pocket and went into this mad act; mumbling to himself, funny walk … the works."

"I guess there are no rules to say tramps can't take photos." I shifted slightly to avoid the damp rocks.

"It wasn't the *camera,* you muppet," said Izzie, exasperated. "It was the act. He was completely different when no one was watching."

"Maybe people spook him."

"That's not all. Last week we went to the Viking Hotel for Dad's birthday. A man came in and sat at the table next to us. He was on his own. He didn't have a beard or long hair like the Eigg man and he was smartly dressed, but I thought I recognised him."

I was getting cold. I moved away from the wall and sat on the edge. Izzie hadn't finished "When he got up to go I took a closer look. Then I *knew* for sure it was him. He has this big mole," she pointed to her forehead. "Here above his right eye. I'm sure it was him."

I thought about what she'd said. "He didn't have a beard, he didn't have long hair and he was smartly dressed but *you* think it was this Eigg man who lives in a cave. *Maybe* he's got a shower in the cave. Maybe he's got his own hairdresser and a designer wardrobe in the cave, too."

Izzie gave me a look. "Listen to me. I've been thinking about this a lot. I know it sounds stupid, but what if it's a false beard and a wig? Clothes are easy to change."

I stared across the blue-black water of the loch to an impressive building, a Leisure Centre and next to it a caravan park. It was as if the loch was a bridge between the old world of this massive stone tower and the new one. The sound of a barking dog drifted across the water.

"So you think he lives in the cave by day and stays at this hotel by night?"

"Aye."

"And you think he's involved with the wildlife smuggling?"

"Aye."

I thought for a minute. I felt a growing excitement. "We could spy on him," I suggested.

"Quick! Get down! There he *is*." Izzie grabbed my arm and pulled me behind the wall. We ducked out of sight.

"If we're going to spy on him, there's no point hiding away," I whispered. I popped my head up. A skinny man, with a thick beard and messy long hair tucked under a baseball cap, was striding along the grass-topped walls. His shabby raincoat billowed out behind him in the wind. He was talking into his hand.

"We can get closer if we keep to the tunnels." I beckoned to Izzie. The whistle of the wind, through the cracks in the walls, changed pitch as we turned a corner.

Because we were down one tier, his boots were at eye level. They were tied with string, muddy and split in the front where his bare toes peeped through. *He must be freezing,* I thought.

He was talking aloud again and, by keeping my back to the wall and moving slightly in front, I could see that he was speaking into a hand-held tape recorder. He coughed to clear his throat.

"Ahem. I'm at Clickimin Broch near Lerwick on the Shetland Isles. In about 1000 BC a Bronze-age family built a small farmhouse on a grassy islet surrounded by loch or marsh, which they walled to enclose their cattle and sheep."

Izzie made an open-palmed gesture at me and raised her shoulders as if to say *"See what I mean?"*

The tramp cleared his throat and spoke again. "The broch was originally between twelve and fifteen metres high, with rooms and staircases. It would have had wooden structures inside, providing shelter for a number of people."

I was sure by his accent that he was from Edinburgh not this Eigg place and he certainly didn't sound mad. I might have heard more except, right at that moment, I tripped over my feet.

"Ouch!" my hands stung where I caught the edge of a stone.

Izzie rushed forward. "Jack?"

The tramp spotted us immediately and the change was startling. His whole body folded in and he pulled the raincoat tightly around him. Mumbling something we couldn't hear he shambled off with a comic limp, leaving us staring after him in amazement.

Izzie was the first to speak. "So what do you think?"

"Um … suspicious, I'll give you that."

"Now what?"

"I don't know. We need evidence or something. We need pictures. I could use one of Mum's cameras." I was beginning to enjoy the idea.

"Why do we need pictures?"

"I dunno … every spy needs pictures, don't they?"

Izzie didn't look so sure. The Eigg man had disappeared over the hill. We ambled back the opposite way, trying to work out a plan. Spying on him was the only thing we could come up with.

Izzie went to check on Octavia, Karma and Bombina. The Clio was parked outside the bungalow so I knew Mum was back. She was sitting having a coffee with Sheila Voss. I was pleased to see her talking to someone. I'd been feeling a bit guilty about leaving her on her own so much.

"Ah, my helper." Sheila said.

Mum was smiling. "Sheila's just explained why the house smelled like a stable when I walked in. Shovelling horse muck? New experience for you, Jack, isn't it?"

I screwed my nose up in disgust. Mum laughed. "Fancy a sandwich?"

"No thanks, we had sausage rolls at Sheila's earlier."

"She's brought this for you." Mum held up a small paperback. "It's her book on the Shetland ponies."

"Thanks," I said.

Sheila shrugged and looked embarrassed. "I meant to give you a copy this morning. You don't have to read it … honestly."

Mum drained her mug of coffee. "So what have you two been up to this afternoon?"

"We went to Clickimin Broch." I helped myself to a packet of crisps and a can of Coke from the fridge.

Sheila turned to Mum. "Jack couldn't have made a better friend on Shetland, Marissa. Izzie is the smartest and most responsible kid I know."

"Well, Jack's no slouch in the brains department either," Mum said proudly. I interrupted quickly before Sheila was made to listen to all my accomplishments since nursery.

"Have you seen the ponies?" I said.

"I certainly have. Aren't they gorgeous? I've taken hundreds of shots." She turned to Sheila. "If you give me your email address, I'll email them to you as soon as we get back home. Another coffee?"

"No thanks," Sheila said getting up. "I've got to go and get ready for my evening surgery. Bye for now. Bye, Jack."

Mum hummed as she rinsed the mugs. It was a tune I recognised, from something called *The*

Four Seasons. I recognised it because it was their favourite tune before ...

Mum seemed to realize what she was humming at the same time and she froze with her back to me.

Her voice quivered as she muttered, "Would you excuse me a minute, Jack?" before running into her room and shutting the door.

I wouldn't let the pain come. I couldn't even though it felt like a huge stone in my chest. I turned the telly on loud and forced myself to watch it.

Mum came out a few minutes later with her eye make up smudged and clutching a tissue.

"I've been thinking," she said, too brightly. "I feel a bit guilty about leaving you on your own so much these last couple of days. I thought we could go out for a meal tonight. Izzie could come too if you like."

I realized that this was the perfect chance to check out Izzie's theory about the mysterious Eigg man. "Can we go to the Viking Hotel?"

"Um ... sure." Mum seemed surprised, whether at my enthusiasm or my choice I don't know.

Mum and Izzie got dressed up. I hardly recognised Izzie with her hair in a ponytail, earrings and a *dress*.

"My mum said I had to make an effort," she explained, but she kept tugging at the hem of the dress and fiddling with her hair. She looked so different I didn't know what to say to her so it was an awkward drive to the hotel with Mum making most of the conversation. But when I tripped getting out of the car Izzie laughed and said, "You might've changed your shoes ... pity you can't change your huge feet."

So I said, "You look like one of Sheila's ponies with your hair like that. Crumble, I think," and we both grinned and then it was okay.

The Viking Hotel was a white, modern rectangle from the outside and red-carpet posh on the inside. The food smelled good and my stomach rumbled. Mum had already booked so we were shown straight to our table by a blond guy who looked as if he worked out a lot; he had that thick neck they get and his suit fitted too snugly over his arms.

"Hello, Louis," Izzie said.

"Izzie, isn't it? Louis said. "My goodness, I hardly recognised you." He turned to Mum "I'm Louis, your waiter for the evening. What can I get for you?"

"Have whatever you want," Mum said to us. "Tonight's my treat." We looked at the menu and ordered. When the waiter left our table I asked Izzie, "Does everyone know everyone else on Shetland?"

"Just about," she nodded her head. "That's the Louis who's renting Sheila's caravan; the guy with the Rottweiler."

"I've never been to such a friendly place," Mum said. "Everyone says hello, even when they don't know you. It's great. You don't get that in the city do you, Jack?"

"No, thank goodness." I said.

We didn't bother with a starter and got stuck

into our main course. Mum had obviously decided not to mention things I didn't want to talk about, so the conversation was easy and fun. Izzie knew everything about anything on Shetland and was more than happy to tell us. I was halfway through a great steak and French fries when Izzie kicked me under the table.

"Ow! Why did you ...?"

She made frantic eye signals to my right. A well-dressed man in his twenties was being shown to the table next to us.

Izzie was nodding and pointing in his direction with her head.

Mum looked worried. "Izzie, what's wrong? Are you okay?"

"Aye, I'm fine. Thank you."

I suddenly remembered why I'd chosen this hotel and took a closer look at the man sitting next to us. He was smart with dark hair and glasses. He didn't look remotely like the shambling misfit I'd seen at Clickimin Broch that afternoon. Louis hurried over to his table. "Good evening, Professor Barr. What can I get for you tonight?"

"Good evening, Louis," the man replied. "How are you?"

"Professor Barr," I mouthed to Izzie.

"A glass of your house wine to start, please, and let's see what you have on your splendid menu," he continued. He *did* have an Edinburgh accent.

Mum looked from me to Izzie and back to me again. "Jack what's going on?"

"Nothing, Mum, Just a case of mistaken identity, that's all."

"Excuse me. I'm just going to the loo," Izzie said. I frowned at her, but she ignored me. As I expected she walked as close to the Professor's table as she possibly could and practically stuck her nose in his face.

She was soon back and before she picked up her knife and fork, she pointed above her right eyebrow to remind me about the mole. I dropped my napkin on the floor so that I could get a better look at the man. She was right about that anyway. The round brown mark was definitely there.

We ate and talked for the rest of the meal but somehow the fun had gone. Izzie was nervous and her eyes kept darting to the next table. After a while I noticed that Professor Barr was staring at us as often as were staring at him.

Izzie struggled through the food on her plate but I ate all mine and managed a chocolate mousse with cream for pudding. Mum had eaten most of her chicken with pink peppercorns and pineapple (which she chose because she said it sounded pretty), and had a Prince Charlie coffee.

When Mum went to pay the bill, Izzie leaned towards me and whispered, "It *is* him. I'm sure."

"It can't be," I said. "He's some sort of professor."

"Who says?" Izzie argued. "Anyway ..."

I felt a tap on my shoulder and I looked up into a pair of dark eyes; dark eyes with glasses and a large mole the size of a currant over the right eyebrow.

He moved in close so that no one else could hear. He smelled like soap. His voice was low and full of menace. "You kids were following me at Clickimin

Broch this afternoon. If you don't stay away from me … you'll regret it. Understand?"

Frightened, we nodded.

It was over in a second and he was heading out of the restaurant, waving a cheerful goodbye to Louis.

I felt my heart banging in my chest and saw that Izzie was scared too. Her face was whiter than the tablecloth.

We had been quiet on the way to the hotel but the journey home was a different kind of silence. Even Mum gave up after a while. "I'm talking to myself here. What's the matter with you two?"

I had visions of the professor, or whoever he was, coming after us in a car and I kept looking behind to check but there were no headlights following us. It was almost eleven o'clock but still light. I would have preferred darkness.

We were only about a mile onto the coast road when the car shuddered and slowed, shuddered again and then stopped.

"Oh no," Mum said.

For one horrible, ridiculous moment I thought, *The professor has arranged this. He's waiting to ambush and murder us all.*

Mum slapped the steering wheel. "Petrol! I forgot to get petrol. Sorry, kids."

"We can call someone," Izzie said. "My mum …"

"Ah, no need. Look at this. Talk about a knight in shining armour." Around the bend came the small white van with the cartoon Shetland ponies painted on the side.

"Sheila!" Izzie shouted.

Mum jumped out of the car and waved frantically. For a minute I thought Sheila was going to drive right past us, but the van slowed and she wound down her window.

"Hello, Good Samaritan," Mum said. "I've run out of petrol."

Izzie and I got out of the car. The sound of the sea was louder than usual. It seemed angry. I hadn't heard it that way before but maybe it was only my mood.

Sheila was looking nervous, annoyed. "Look. I can't stop right now. I have to go. I have … um … an emergency. Izzie, you must know someone you can call?"

The sea boomed against the shore again. Mum took a couple steps back, obviously hurt and puzzled by Sheila's manner.

"Yeah, we can phone my mum. Sheila, are you okay?"

"I've got to go," Sheila said. "I'm sorry I …" and she drove off leaving the three of us just standing there.

Izzie was the first to speak. "It must be a real emergency," she said almost apologetically.

Izzie used Mum's mobile to call her mother and we sat on the grass waiting. We were silent again. I picked at a few blades of grass and tossed them into the wind. The sea boomed on the rocks below. Luckily, we didn't have to wait long and Mrs Christie's Fiat van drove towards us, its radiator shining like a big metal smile. I was surprised to see it was blue not yellow.

"So you ran out of petrol, Mrs McKenzie."

"Call me Marissa, please," Mum said. "I'm so sorry about this."

"And I'm Denise. Not to worry, dear. We'll have you home in no time."

We piled into the van. Mum sat in the passenger seat and Izzie and I slid the door across and climbed into the back. I wondered why there was such a big space inside with no seats but soon figured out it must be for Mr Christie's wheelchair.

"And did you have a pleasant evening?" Mrs Christie said.

"Lovely."

"Great food."

"Very nice." I realized it *had* been a good evening until the threats from the nutty professor. Mrs Christie's chatter cheered us up and before we got home we were even laughing again.

"I'll pick you up in the morning and we'll get some petrol and go fetch your car. It'll be quite safe where it is for the night," Mrs Christie told Mum.

Mum gave me a hug goodnight and went straight to bed but I listened to my music for a while. I knew I wouldn't sleep, there was too much on my mind.

If this professor guy was really the same person as the Eigg man — as Izzie called him — then he was certainly up to something. Judging by his reaction, it was something very serious too. I wondered if we should call the police.

I still felt a bit peckish so I got a Mars Bar from the fridge. The black leather sofa squeaked when I threw myself full length on it. But what could we tell the police? Please sir, we think there's a man who dresses up as a tramp. They'd have a good laugh at that.

My mind went round in circles and came up with nothing. I stuffed the last of the Mars Bar into my mouth and went to bed.

I couldn't sleep, and this time it wasn't just the light. The battery had run down on my iPod and I needed something to take my mind off Professor Psycho in the Viking Hotel.

I reached over to the bedside cupboard and picked up Sheila's book entitled *The Life and Times of the Shetland Pony from the 1800s to the Millennium.*

"Catchy!" I said sarcastically. I kicked off my shoes, puffed up my pillow and lay, still dressed, on the bed.

In the 1800s, I read, *Shetlands were imported in great numbers to haul coal cars in the "pits." Many of these ponies were born and died in the mines. Some never saw the light of day. At the end of their shift, the men went up to the surface to be with their families, but apart from a brief "holiday" once a year, the ponies stayed underground all the time.*

The book wasn't helping. The thought of ponies living their whole lives in the dark made me miserable to think that they never saw a cloud or felt sunshine or rolled in the grass like Sheila's ponies. They never even tasted a mint.

I knelt on the bed and looked out of the window. Two sheep and a brown-coloured pony were on the beach nibbling seaweed off the rocks. I hadn't known that animals ate seaweed. Then I saw the flicker again; a fire and a dark figure huddled close to it, warming its hands. I grabbed the binoculars and focused them, recognising the huge red and black biker boots immediately. Slasher. I ducked down out of sight, my heart beating. I didn't know if he could see into my window but I wasn't taking any chances. What was Slasher doing on the beach? For the next few minutes crazy thoughts flashed through my mind. Was he after revenge for his boots? Was he coming for me? Had he found out where I was and was waiting with his blood-soaked dagger for me to show myself?

Gradually, my hand stopped shaking and I took another look through the binoculars. Slasher was propped against a rock, spooning baked beans straight from a can into his mouth. He was smiling, looking happy and relaxed. He didn't look like a man on a murder mission. I was being stupid. He wasn't after me at all. It was just a coincidence he had chosen this beach. Anyway, after the threats from the tramp-professor, at the Viking Hotel, Slasher didn't seem so sinister any more. Maybe he just liked beaches at night. Maybe he liked his own company, maybe … ah, who cared. I flopped back onto my duvet and picked up the book again.

In some mines, the men drew lots to decide who worked with each pony. They would then stay together, working side by side, for months. My eyes felt heavy and I forced them to carry on reading. *Real affection existed between the men and their charges. There are stories of men saved from cave-ins by a bolting pony. Loyalty ran deep in the pits and …*

I must have fallen asleep because I dreamed that I had a Shetland pony of my own. He was red and brown with a thick curly mane and a mole above his right eye. But when I tried to stroke him he turned into a massive spider with eight hairy legs and scuttled down a mine.

5. Coves and caves

"If he is smuggling live animals, we won't let him get away with it," I told the cross-eyed koala. I fiddled with my hair. My fringe needed cutting. It was hanging over my eyes like a Shetland pony's mane.

We could get some photos, I thought, *and take them to the police.* Izzie's uncle was a policeman. He'd know what to do.

It was still early so I had another Mars bar for breakfast before Mum got up and nagged me into having a fruit smoothie or that sawdust stuff she called muesli.

Izzie was already in her zoo. "Hold Karma, will you? I need to give his cage a good clean." She lifted the chameleon gently onto the back of my hand. "Stand still. No sudden moves or you'll stress him," she warned.

Stress him? I thought, but managed a weak smile in reply.

He was quite cute; like a little triceratops with three horns on his head. But his eyes were freaky; they moved independently, one was looking at me and the other at my hand. His feet felt like spiky twigs.

"Does he bite?" I talked through the side of my mouth so I wouldn't move too much and disturb him.

"Only on a Tuesday," Izzie said.

"Oh, ha ha."

She pulled out the old branches and wiped the cage clean with paper towels. Fresh branches went in and she sprayed the leaves before taking Karma from me. Holding him against her neck in a hug for a minute before putting him back, she carried the cage nearer to the window so that he could get some natural light, chatting to him as she worked.

I thought of the girls in my class with their giggling, their sparkly mobiles and their pop magazines. And I thought how *different* Izzie was.

I heard Mum calling, "Jack? Jack?"

"Shut the shed door behind you," Izzie whispered.

I nodded. "I'm here, Mum. One sec."

Mum was shouting over the bush that divided our bungalow from Izzie's cottage.

"Mrs Christie is taking me to the petrol station and then to get the car. We may do a spot of shopping while we're gone. She said to tell you Mr Christie is there if you need anything."

"Okay."

"I've got a surprise for you. I've booked a trip for this afternoon … to the island of Mousa, on a boat."

"A boat? Do you really think after what happened on the ferry, that I'll enjoy a boat trip?"

"Don't worry. It's not the same. This is a small boat and it only takes fifteen minutes to get to the island."

I wasn't convinced but was too agitated to argue. "Can I borrow a camera while you're gone?"

"Sure. Use the Canon but be careful with it, please. Make sure you're back here by one thirty at the latest if you go out. The boat leaves at two."

"Yeah, fine, see you later."

Neither Izzie nor I had mentioned the Professor and what he'd said to us the night before, but it was obvious we were both thinking about it. I spoke first.

"He shouldn't get away with it," I said. "I've got a camera. All we need is proof."

Izzie's eyes were steely, more silvery than I'd ever seen them. "Let's do it," she replied.

"Are you scared?" I said.

"Terrified. You?"

"Yeah."

I sprayed Bombina while Izzie changed Octavia's water. The tarantula hadn't moved much but she looked better somehow; brighter and perkier. The hairs on her legs were fluffier too.

"We can use my computer to print out the photos *if* I can get Dad off it for long enough, 'cos he sells his boats in bulbs on eBay. And Mum plays online bingo when she can't get to the bingo night in Lerwick"

"What?"

She smiled, easing the tension. "I know. It's an island thing. She's really good at it, too. Wins something most weeks."

Before we left, Izzie went into her house and came back wearing a red and yellow hoodie and carrying two of her dad's white handkerchiefs, which she tucked them into her jeans pocket.

"We'll need these," she said.

"What for?"

"You'll find out," she said mysteriously.

On that particular Tuesday morning, Shetland was misty. The hills were covered with a ghostly fog. We walked along the coast road with the sea splashing to our left and the sound of trickling water, in the damp earth, on our right. I told Izzie about Slasher being outside her house the night before, but she didn't make much of it.

"So? Loads of people camp on the beach … even in May! It's this next cove. There's a cave there. We'll have to get close. Be careful. It's a really steep cliff," Izzie warned.

The noise of the seabirds was deafening. We had to shout above the screaming as they dived from the cliffs into the waves, or skimmed the razor edge of rocks to land on ledges no wider than my hand.

A few feet away, leaning against a boulder were several canes about a metre long. "We'll each need one of these," Izzie said. "You'll soon find out why."

We lay belly-down on the crunchy grass, slithered to the edge and looked onto the cove below. Izzie pointed and shouted over the birds, "That's the cave he stays in … there."

The entrance was no more than a metre-wide, narrow slit in the rocks. It was impossible to see inside but if someone was living in there, it must have been pretty dark. We watched for a while but I was soon distracted by the comings and goings of the birds.

Izzie punched my arm. "There he is."

I fumbled the camera out of its case and pressed a few buttons trying to look like I knew what I was doing. Below us, on the beach was the tall slim figure of the Eigg man. It was hard to believe that the smart guy at the Viking Hotel could be the same person as the scruffy tramp. If he and the professor *weren't* the same man, then taking a couple of pictures wouldn't hurt. If it *was* him then we would have some sort of evidence.

The sea spray misted the lens, and making out the fuzzy shape in the viewfinder proved difficult. He seemed to be collecting shells; picking them up, examining them, putting some in his pocket and letting others fall back onto the beach.

"Take a picture … quickly!" Izzie shouted impatiently. I raised myself up onto my knees and felt the tremor in my legs as I realized how close I was to the edge of the cliff. I squinted into the viewfinder, zoomed in, focused and clicked … and the flash went off.

The professor or Eigg man — whoever he was — saw the flash and looked up at us. For a few seconds we just stared at each other. Then he sprinted up the cliff path towards us with terrifying speed.

"*Run*!"

Izzie didn't need telling twice. She bolted across the top of the cliff. "Grab your stick," she shouted at me.

I hesitated, confused.

Izzie looked up at the sky, turned back towards me and screamed again, "Get it … quickly."

The enormous skuas, angry at our intrusion

to their nesting ground, attacked. Swooping like dive-bombers, they dropped towards us, striking out with their wings and feet. It was terrifying. I scrambled away from them, trying to protect my head, while sprinting back along the cliff to grab the cane I'd left lying in the grass.

The birds dived again, screaming their anger. A claw ripped at my hair catching my forehead and I felt a sharp sting. I stumbled backwards, closer to the cliff edge.

I grabbed my stick and beat at the air. Izzie had tied one of her father's hankies to hers and it was working; the violent swoops centred now on the white flag. In all the confusion, I'd almost forgotten the Eigg man but at that moment he appeared on the cliff top, panting and red-faced.

"Come here, you!"

We ran, slapping the air to fight off the crazed birds. We must have looked really stupid, running with long sticks like white flags, as if we were surrendering ... but they kept the birds away and the skies above us gradually emptied.

The Eigg man wasn't so lucky. He didn't have a stick or a handkerchief. The birds swooped down on him screaming with fury, battering his face and head with the full strength of their wings and beaks. We stopped behind a boulder and, bent double, tried to catch our breath. Five birds attacked at once. The man tried to shield his face with his arms but it was no use. He was screaming at the birds, calling for help and then he fell to the ground and lay still. The skuas veered off in triumph.

"He's hurt," Izzie said.

"What are you doing?"

"I'm going to help him."

"Don't be ridiculous."

"He's *hurt.*" She was already running back towards him.

"Izzie, don't be stupid. It could be a trick … Izzie! Oh damn!" I ran after her.

The skuas had drifted away but their *Gek-Gek* screams of victory echoed across the cliffs. Izzie reached him before me. She knelt down on the grass beside him. Immediately his hand shot out as fast as a snake strike and grabbed her ankle.

"Gotcha," he said. There was a nasty smile on his face.

Izzie screamed. She struggled and tried to pull away.

"Let her go," I shouted. I struck out with the cane and caught him a stinging blow to his legs. Izzie kicked with her free leg.

"Ow! Ouch, stop it!" he shouted.

"I'll get the police," I yelled.

What the Eigg man said next was the last thing I expected to hear, "Calm down … calm down, will you? I *am* the police."

That stopped us in our tracks.

"If I let go, will you promise not to run away?"

Izzie nodded. I said, "No."

"Look, I'm telling the truth. Let me show you. I've got my identification here." He fumbled in his pocket and for one scary second I thought he was going to pull out a gun like they do on the telly. So, I whacked him again.

"Ow! Will you *stop!*" He tried to hand me a card.

I wouldn't take it. I was sure he'd grab my arm if I did.

"Let her go!"

He let go of Izzie's leg but she didn't run away. She seemed to be listening to him. "I'm really sorry about last night. I didn't want you involved." He tried to get up and I whacked his leg with the cane again.

"Agh. Unless you want to be charged with assaulting a police officer, you'd better stop that right now."

He threw the card on the ground beside me. Still holding the stick like a weapon, I picked it up. It said Quincy Barr. NWCU. Lothian and Borders Police.

"I'm with the National Wildlife Crime Unit, based at North Berwick police station. Look, if you don't believe me, you can contact Sergeant Duncan Christie here in Lerwick. He knows me well.

"Unca Dunc?" Izzie sounded surprised.

"What?"

"That's my Uncle Duncan."

"Well, there you are then. Check with him." The Eigg man's wig had come loose and was tilted down over his eyebrows. He looked even more scared than I felt. He was still lying flat on the ground and he held up his hands in a surrender signal.

"So you're not a professor?"

"No, I just thought it sounded good. Can I get up now, *please?*" he said. "Then I'll explain everything."

Although the entrance was narrow the cave opened out into a fair sized room. It was dry inside and we huddled around the warmth of the petrol stove.

"Make yourselves comfortable on the sleeping bag. I'll take the deckchair," he said. "I can get rid of these now." He pulled off the wig with a flourish and then tried the same with the false beard. "Ow, ow, ow," he muttered as it peeled away from his chin. It left a red mark around his mouth. "That really hurts. Gets me every time." He rubbed his face. "As you seem to be on to me ... at least partly ... I've decided to tell you everything. But you've got to promise not to tell a soul. It's really important. More than that ... it's crucial."

We both nodded.

"I'm going to have to trust you. Can I trust you?"

We nodded again.

The stone ceiling was about seven feet above our heads, the walls had rusty streaks with the odd branch of dried seaweed stuck to them. From the entrance to about three feet in, the floor was painted a thick white with birds' droppings. On a First Aid box Quincy's collection of shells was arranged neatly by size.

"I'll make some tea, shall I? Or would you prefer a pot noodle?" Izzie said tea, I said pot noodle.

"Spicy curry or chicken and mushroom?" He held up the two choices.

"Umm ... chicken and mushroom, please."

Inside the cave the water boiled with a gentle hiss and outside, the sea slurped and slapped against the rocks.

"I'm undercover," he said. "More than that, actually, I'm also on my own time. As I told you I work for the NWCU which is part of the Lothian and Borders Police. We're a special unit set up to help combat, among other things, the illegal trade in wildlife."

Izzie and I looked at each other.

Quincy intercepted the look. "I see you know something about this."

Izzie leaned forward "My Uncle's Duncan Christie, remember? He came to my school to talk about it."

"Then he must have told you that hundreds of millions of plants and animals, worth billions of pounds, are traded each year, and that this has a direct effect on the survival of some species."

I got the feeling that this was a speech Quincy had made lots of times. His anger was real though, that's for sure. I could see it in his eyes.

"Our research shows that the UK is a major player in the illegal trade. Thousands of seizures are made at ports and airports, and shops across the country are selling some of the world's most endangered species. It's a disgrace"

He poured boiling water from the pan into a mug and added a tea bag. "I haven't got any sugar or milk, I'm afraid."

"That's okay." Izzie took the tea from him and blew on the surface.

"There's big money to be made in this trade, make no mistake. Two Lear's macaws are worth more than an "S-class" Mercedes and, ounce for ounce, Shahtoosh shawls, made from the wool of the Tibetan antelope, are worth more than gold." He filled the pot noodle and handed it to me along with a Swiss army knife.

"Thanks." I eased out one metal tool after another until I found a spoon. "Aren't you having anything?"

"I had a very nice four-course breakfast at The Viking," he smiled. "We know that one of the most used ports is Lerwick. We also know that there's a gang regularly operating out of here. I want to stop them."

A sudden squall of wind blew in from the cave entrance and the flames of the camping stove flickered but didn't go out.

"This disguise," he lifted the ends of his shabby coat, "is so that I can move around Shetland without arousing too much curiosity. We're pretty sure we're already onto one of the gang, but we don't know who Mr Big is. We think the ringleader has either lived here for a long time or is a Shetlander. You locals are friendly but also loyal to each other."

"I'm not a local," I said. "I'm from Edinburgh."

"Really?" Quincy's face lit up. "Me too … Marchmont."

"So much for your Eigg man," I said to Izzie.

"Egg man?" Quincy said looking puzzled.

"I'm from Abbey Hill," I said.

"Hibernian FC?"

"*Forever!*" I said enthusiastically.

I put my pot noodle down and Quincy and I did a high five.

Izzie groaned and rolled her eyes. "If you're done with the male bonding can we get on?"

Quincy coughed and sat back on the deckchair. "Where was I? Oh yes. If you see or hear anything suspicious, let me know."

"Tell him about Octavia," I said to Izzie. She frowned and shook her head.

"Who's Octavia?" Quincy asked.

"Tell him," I said.

Quincy misunderstood her reluctance. "Don't underestimate the cruelty of these people, Izzie. They're not the least bit interested in the welfare of the animals. We raided a taxidermist shop in London and found two stuffed tiger cubs, a gorilla skull, a leopard, an elephant's foot and tusk ... those animals were slaughtered for ornaments."

"Don't," Izzie said, close to tears.

"*Tell* him," I said.

"We found a live tarantula," Izzie said.

The effect on Quincy was like an electric shock. "What? Where?" He shot up out of the deckchair.

"Saturday. In my bungalow," I said and told him where I was staying.

"Damn! They've done it again. Damn them! Right under my nose." He kicked over a plastic water bottle. The liquid trickled out and pooled in a corner and seeped into the sand. "They're so cunning. You wouldn't believe the tricks they get up to. It makes it so tough for us. We've found rhino horns hidden in statues, suitcases filled with rare birds stuffed into tubes. I even caught one smuggler wearing a live snake like a belt." He calmed down a little but still paced the cave. "So, they must have landed near your house. The tarantula couldn't have made it far in this cold weather," he said. "I know that cove. It's got some decent rock cover. I'm assuming the spider is dead now?"

"No," Izzie said. "Octavia's fine. She's a *Brachypelma smithi;* a Mexican red-kneed tarantula."

Quincy was obviously impressed. "You know your spiders, Izzie."

"I know my creatures," she replied. "I've looked after her. She's lovely. I don't want her taken away from me."

Quincy hesitated. His eyebrows met over his eyes in a frown, the large mole over his right eye dipped towards his nose.

"Has either of you told anyone about this tarantula?"

"No," we said together.

"Then, don't. It's not just a pet, Izzie. What you have is evidence. Look, I can't emphasize too much how dangerous these people are. They have a great deal to lose; their freedom as well as their money. They won't let a couple of kids stand in their way. Do you understand what I'm saying?"

Izzie and I looked at each other and nodded. I suddenly wasn't hungry any more and placed the pot noodle on the cave floor with the Swiss army knife beside it.

Izzie sipped her tea. Her hands cupped around it for warmth.

"Can I come to see your ... um, Octavia?" Quincy asked. "Don't worry. If you're looking after her properly, and I think I can assume you are, I'll make sure you keep her. I think you may have given me a really important clue to our Mr

Big," he added thoughtfully. "Can I come later this afternoon?"

"Afternoon?" Izzie shot up from the sleeping bag, looking at her watch. "Jack, you're going to Mousa. You're late."

"Come tomorrow morning," I shouted over my shoulder to Quincy as we hurtled out of the cave. "Meet us at Izzie's house. It's next door to where I'm staying."

"Jack, come on!" Izzie shouted, already further ahead.

6. Pig fish

"Jack, we'll miss the boat!" Mum was shouting. "Is that blood on your forehead? Look at the state of you. You've got mud all over your clothes. Well it's too late to shower or change now. Just get in the car."

Irritated, I climbed into the passenger seat and slammed the door shut. "I don't want to go on another dumb boat trip. It'll be your fault if I'm sick again." Mum was driving too fast and as we took the next corner a sheep bolted out of the way, just in time.

"Muuum!"

"Sorry," she said and immediately slowed down. "It's just … this holiday together … It's not working out the way I'd hoped it would."

I didn't answer her. Unclipping the glove compartment I helped myself to a packet of wine gums. Mum held her hand out and I dropped an orange one into her palm.

"So what happened to your head?"

I flipped the sun visor down and peered into the mirror. "It's just a scratch … a bird did it?"

"A bird?"

"Yes, a Bonxie," I said, using the local name.

"Never heard of one of those," Mum laughed.

"We were on the cliff by their nesting ground. They really didn't like it and they attack people. Someone leaves big sticks there for people to protect themselves. Izzie tied hankies to our sticks and it worked. Well ... almost." I rubbed at the scratch with my finger. I said nothing about Quincy and the animal smuggling. He'd told us not to anyway.

"There it is," Mum said. A signpost pointed to Sandwick. It was easy to find the Leebitton slip-way. Since there are no trees on Shetland, places stand out, so you can see them long before you get to them. Beside a group of buildings with red doors, the boat was moored, bobbing gently on the water. I felt happier when I realized we could actually see Mousa island from the shore. No long trip this time then. The water seemed calm enough too so I crossed my fingers and hoped.

The *Bateau IV* was ready to leave and the boatman pointed at his watch and beckoned for us to hurry. Mum parked, locked the car and we stumbled across the rocks to get aboard.

The first chug of the engines made my stomach churn with memory but as soon as the boatman began talking about the wildlife and history, I became so engrossed that I forgot about feeling sick.

Within minutes, someone shouted and pointed at the water.

"Yes, a porpoise," the boatman said calmly as if porpoises were an everyday kind of thing, which, thinking about it, they probably were to him. "Mousa Sound is one of the best places in Britain to see them. The habit they have of coming to the surface and making a snorting noise has given rise to different names. The latin name was *Porcus piscus* or 'pig fish' as it translates today."

Cameras clicked and I saw Mum fighting with a tangle of leads in her backpack to get to her telescopic lens.

"We call them 'Neesicks' from the Norse word *nisa* – it means to sneeze." I was enjoying these weird words and thinking about maybe even writing them down, when I saw him.

He was on the other side of the boat. His great tattooed arms bulging out of the sleeves of a red T-shirt like legs of mutton. My eyes were automatically drawn down to the deck and his red and black boots.

"Slasher!" I said out loud and immediately wished I hadn't. He turned but I was quicker. I tugged at the hood of my jacket pulled it down over my face like a Jedi Knight.

"Jack?" Mum was looking at me with her worried face.

"Shhh," I hissed at her. "That's the guy on the ferry. The one I was sick on."

"Well, maybe now would be a good time to apologize."

"No … he'll eat me."

"Don't be ridiculous," Mum whispered back. There was another yelp of excitement as two dark heads surfaced, looking directly at us.

"Common seals," said the boatman. "If we're lucky we'll see some greys by the pools on Mousa. It's a bit early for the pups yet, though."

The seals were funny; like dogs with whiskers and no ears. They weren't a bit afraid and swam close to the boat watching us, watching them.

I was enjoying myself until I heard the clunk

of buckles as Slasher clomped towards me, "Hey, aren't you ...?"

I thought my luck had just run out when someone screamed, "Look! A Whale!" I forgot about Slasher in a second and rushed with everyone else to the other side of the boat. Mum shoved a pair of binoculars into my hand.

Black and white and enormous, it turned and fell and re-entered the water in a graceful belly-flop; its huge tail fin was the last thing to disappear into the ripples. I realized I'd been holding my breath and blew out between my lips. There was a stunned silence on the boat until a man said "Wow!" And everyone started talking at once.

Mum was wide-eyed with joy. "I got it," she said holding up her camera. "I got a magnificent shot. What a sight. Glad you came now?"

"Phew. You bet."

"Aren't you going ashore, lad?" The boatman was holding out a hand to help me off.

"Yes. Yes." I'd waited until Slasher went ahead. I could see him striding along the path. His leather jacket slung over his shoulder.

Mum had met another photographer on the boat and she was walking beside him talking excitedly about lenses and camera angles.

"The Northern Lights," I heard her say.

"A photographer's dream," the man said. "I've been coming here for years but I've only caught them once. I'll never forget it, though. Stunning. Simply stunning."

I thought again how tiny mum was, how young she looked. She could almost have passed for one of my school friends. I trailed behind feeling a bit left out and wishing Izzie was there. She had a way of making everything more interesting ... more alive.

Mousa Broch was cool. Much higher than the broch at Clickimin that Izzie had shown me. It just got bigger and bigger the closer we got. Someone was reading out loud from a tourist book and said it was fifteen metres across on the outside but, because the walls were so thick, only six metres on the inside.

We stood at the bottom of the broch and looked up through the great stone tower." I can't imagine people living here, can you?" I said.

Mum shook her head.

I wanted to explore on my own so Mum handed me a pack of sandwiches from her backpack and a bottle of water. She saw me frown and said, "You've been eating and drinking far too much rubbish lately." I couldn't exactly argue.

There were small stone rooms like dungeons everywhere and a steep narrow staircase led up and up. I couldn't resist that. Higher up, the tower passages ran between the inner and outer walls. It was like some Stone-age play centre. I reached a kind of landing about halfway up and decided it was a good place for a picnic. I tucked myself into a crevice. The sandwiches were lettuce and tomato on wholemeal bread.

"Terrific," I said. But if you didn't count the Mars bar, and I didn't, I'd had nothing to eat apart from half a pot noodle with Quincy. I was starving.

I squeezed into a corner and began to eat and as I ate, I went over the last few days in my mind. So ... Izzie and I were rubbish detectives. The man we thought was the smuggler had turned out to be the guy *chasing* the smuggler. It was pretty exciting while it lasted though.

I thought about whacking Quincy's legs with the stick. It had been good of him not to make a fuss about that. He could have arrested me, I suppose. I bet his legs were sore though. So, if Quincy wasn't the smuggler, who was Mr Big?

I heard voices echoing through the chambers and footsteps climbing the stairs. I curled up against the wall and two women and a man passed without seeing me. Finishing the sandwich, I took a long swig of water. It actually tasted quite good.

A metal railing circled the opening at the top and made a walkway right around. The view was stunning; I could see far out across the island and the water. The wind made a whistling sound and I shivered. I was going into a daydream gazing out over sea when a voice bellowed.

"Hey, kid ..."

Slasher. I popped back into the opening with the speed of a rabbit down its hole. I was hurtling down the steps so fast, it's a wonder I didn't break my neck. I almost fell out of the entrance and barrelled straight into Mum and the other photographer.

"Jack. Steady. What's wrong?" She put her hand on my shoulder.

"Nothing," I said, my eyes glued to the entrance,

waiting for the loony biker to race out after me. He didn't.

"Time to get back to the boat," Mum said. I followed her and the photographer back to the landing stage. We saw the grey seals splashing in the pool but I was too nervous watching out for Slasher to enjoy them.

The trip back to the mainland was less eventful than the trip out. The same two seals made an appearance but nothing else did. I made sure I stayed with the other people on the boat. I pulled my hood up again but was sure I could feel Slasher's eyes on me.

As soon as we got back to the house Izzie was knocking on our door. "Mum and Dad said would you like to come to a barbecue in the garden this evening?"

"That would be lovely, thank you." Mum said.

I showered and changed. The excitement of the day still showed in Mum's eyes and it made me happy to see her like that for once.

The sound of the fiddle started as we pushed our way past the prickly bush and into the Christie's garden. Mr Christie was in his wheelchair on the patio, playing a sad tune that seemed to float out over the sea.

Mrs Christie bustled in and out of the house carrying trays of food and drinks to the table. She was wearing a bright yellow dress that matched her kitchen walls perfectly. Burgers and sausages frizzled on a barbecue and the smoky charcoal smell made my mouth water.

"Ah, Marissa, Jack. Welcome. Why don't you sit

down here. We've got lots of food and plenty to drink."

Mum handed her two bottles of wine.

"Oh, you shouldn't have, dear. It's one of my bingo barbecues. Any winnings over sixty pounds go towards a nice evening." She kissed Mum on the cheek.

Izzie shoved a hotdog in my hand; it was perfect and even more perfect with a long squirt of ketchup. I was starving again after the Mousa trip and got stuck in.

"You'll never guess what happened this afternoon?" We were sitting on a blanket Mrs Christie had laid over a grassy bank.

"What?" Izzie looked at me.

"Slasher, that's what! He was on the boat trip to Mousa and I *know* he's after me now."

"Are you *still* going on about that guy you threw up over?"

"Yeah, but you don't have to keep mentioning the sick thing. He was definitely following me and shouted at me as soon as we were alone."

"Oh come on, you're imagining it. It's not as if you wanted to chuck up on his new boots." She flipped the ring pull on her Coke, "Unless he's some sort of sicko." She took a swig but it immediately sprayed out of her mouth and nose as she snorted with laughter. "Sicko. Get it? Sicko."

"Oh very funny, Ha ha ha."

Just then the gate opened and Sheila arrived with a man I'd not seen before.

"Unca Dunc!" Izzie jumped up and ran to meet him. She threw her arms around him in a big hug.

"I haven't seen you for days."

"No, we've had a lot on lately. How's my favourite girl?"

"This is Jack," she introduced me. "Jack, this is my Uncle Duncan."

"Or 'Unca Dunc' as she's called me since she was two."

Izzie looked embarrassed. The family likeness was strong and I would easily have guessed that he was a relation. His silver-coloured eyes were wider and his hair not quite so thick and crinkly but the rest of his face was identical to his brother's.

Sheila waved a glass of wine at us and we waved back.

It was clear that Mr Christie was as pleased to see his brother as Izzie was. His smile lit up his whole his face "Well, get out that ol' fiddle of yours, man. We'll duel with the devil tonight."

From then on the music was faster, louder and happier as the two brothers played. They only stopped to take sips of beer between tunes. Sometimes they sang songs too and then Izzie, Sheila and Mrs Christie joined in. I was soon clapping and beating time with my foot along with the rest of them. It was great music, wild music; music that made your heart beat. I watched in fascination as the men's bows and fingers blurred with speed as the fiddle notes rose over the sound of the waves. When they stopped it was like a light had gone out.

"Phew. I'd like to play guitar like that."

"What ... with a bow?" Izzie said.

"No stupid, I mean ..."

"I know what you mean," she said. "They're great, aren't they?" And her voice was full of pride. I helped myself to a third hotdog and we sat back on the blanket. Minx padded over, climbed onto Izzie's lap and settled down purring softly.

"What happened to your Dad?"

"You mean the wheelchair?"

"Yes.

"He has MS … multiple sclerosis." She saw my blank look. "It's a condition that can affect different parts of the body. In Dad it's his legs. He was fine until he was about thirty-five." I saw tears gather in her eyes and wished I hadn't asked. She wiped her eyes and sniffed.

"What about *your* dad? You never mention him."

The question shouldn't have caught me unawares but it did. The pain was like the kick of a horse. I tried to swallow a lump of hotdog but it stuck in my throat. I coughed and Izzie handed me her can of Coke.

Then, out of nowhere, I said, "Oh, my Dad is the coolest guy. You'll love him when you meet him. Everyone does." The pain eased immediately and I found myself telling Izzie all about Gerald Ian McKenzie. My dad. The words slipped out naturally. It didn't feel like lying.

"He'd be here with us now but he's on a job in Dubai. I told him about the tarantula and he thinks it's really cool. Dad's into wildlife. He's a member of the World Wildlife Fund."

Now that I'd started it was like a flood. I told her how he'd taught me to snorkel and how he cheated at computer games by nudging me when I was winning. I told her he was allergic to prawns and would only wear blue shoes. I told her he called Mum "Rissie," and how he'd collected air-sickness bags from every flight he'd ever been on. I couldn't *stop* talking and I saw Izzie was relieved when her uncle joined us. It was like I'd been under some sort of spell; a spell that made me happy for a short while, but I was awake again now and my heart thudded uncomfortably.

Izzie's uncle handed out biscuits. "You've got to try this, lad. Izzie's mother makes the best butter shortbread for miles."

"Do you know Quincy Barr?" Izzie asked him.

He looked at us, suspiciously. "Sure, I know Quince? How come you do?"

Izzie lowered her voice. "So he really is a policeman with the National Wildlife Crime Unit and he's undercover to catch criminals smuggling wildlife into Lerwick?"

There was a sound like a sneeze and I saw Sheila standing just behind us holding a glass of wine.

"Where's the fiddler? We want more music," she said, laughing.

"Be there in a sec," Izzie's uncle stood up. He waited for Sheila to move away then said, "We'll talk about this later. I don't know what Quincy has told you but keep out of it, do you understand? These are dangerous people we're dealing with."

Izzie nodded and I did too. Suddenly, it didn't seem so much like a game. We were both silent until the fiddle music started again. It was impossible to feel bad when the music played. It was a thrilling, dancing tune and we were soon clapping and swirling around with the others.

The brightness of the evening meant I had no idea what time it was. I'd hated the hours and hours of light but now I liked it. It made me feel there was more time somehow. Above the whoops of delight, as the music got faster, I told Izzie about the whale.

"You're lucky," she said. "I've only seen a whale about a dozen times myself. I've seen loads of seals, of course. I had a pet one for a few years. It kept coming back and it got so tame I could feed it by hand."

"What are we going to do about Quincy?"

"Do?" she shrugged. "I'm not going to do anything. He's coming here tomorrow to see Octavia. It's too late to stop him now, isn't it?"

"Yes, but we could ..."

I was interrupted by a scream from Izzie. "What are you doing!" She jumped up, forgetting about Minx in her lap and the cat dropped to the ground with yowl.

She'd screamed so loudly, her father and uncle stopped playing and everyone looked at her.

"I didn't say you could go in there!" She was shouting at Sheila Voss who had unlocked the shed door and was about to make her way inside. Izzie was beside her in a flash and slammed the door closed.

"I just thought I'd take a look at Bombina and Karma while I was here." Sheila was obviously shaken by Izzie's behaviour.

Mrs Christie hurried over, still holding a coffee

pot in her hand, “Izzie what on earth? If Sheila wants to take a look at your little pets, you should be grateful.”

Izzie stood with her back against the shed door. She didn’t say a word. Her face was pale and her eyes looked more silver than ever. I really admired her guts.

Everyone looked awkward and no one spoke. At last, Sheila walked away, making a weak joke about Izzie having a strong, protective instinct.

Mrs Christie was angry. “What was that all about, miss?”

“Nothing.”

It was all over in a few minutes but it changed the tone of the evening. The Christie brothers played a quiet, sad song and Sheila left early, saying, “No, really it was fine,” and “of course Izzie hadn’t upset her.”

“I couldn’t let her find Octavia could I?” Izzie was close to tears.

“No. You couldn’t.” I whispered back.

Mum and I left soon after. We were both tired out.

“Night, Jack. That was a pretty good day all in all, don’t you think?”

“All in all,” I agreed. “Night, Mum.”

Slasher was there again, in his usual place, huddled over his campfire. From behind the bedroom curtains I trained the binoculars on him. I could see he’d collected a few things to make himself more comfortable. A small saucepan rested on the fire, heating something, soup or maybe water for coffee. What looked like a sleeping bag was rolled up beside him. He'd taken off his black and red boots and they balanced on a rock glowing in the pink light.

He stood up and I ducked behind the curtain. I didn't know what to think about Slasher any more. Izzie was right. He wouldn't be stalking me unless he was some psycho. But then again he did chase me — kind of — at Mousa. I plugged my iPod in to charge the battery and picked up the binoculars again.

But if he was after me why did he just sit on the beach all night and disappear before I got up? It didn't make any sense.

I was tired. Too tired to even think about it. I was starting to enjoy the quiet and the sound of the sea. The gentle swish made me sleepy. Before long, I was fast asleep.

I woke in the early hours and sat bolt upright. What a muppet I was! It was obvious. Why hadn't I thought of it before?

I jumped out of bed, grabbed the binoculars and peered outside. But it was too dark to see anything. Not even the glimmer of a bonfire.

7. The bundle on the beach

I was so excited that I was out of bed before Mum woke, pacing up and down the bungalow waiting for a reasonable time to go and call for Izzie. At seven, I took Mum a cup of coffee and frightened her to death.

"Jack, what is it? What's wrong?"

"Nothing's wrong. I can bring my mother a cup of coffee, can't I?"

"You never have before."

"Well if you don't want it ..."

"No, no. It's great. Thank you." She took a sip and squinted at her watch. Her eyebrows went up. "Are you sure nothing's wrong?"

"I thought you might like a lie in this morning, that's all."

"Do you know what, oh son of mine? I rather think I would." She pulled the duvet over her head with a long sigh.

It was the first time I'd been into Mum's room and I saw it hadn't escaped the Oz theme. There was a map over the bed and several flags dotted about. A poster of a fat bird with a big head was blu-tacked to the side of the wardrobe. I didn't recognize it, but it was a sure bet it came from Australia. *Izzie probably knew the name of the bird, the species and the Latin name for it too,* I thought.

I lasted until eight and then I went and knocked on Izzie's door. She was already up and dressed.

"I'm just going to sort out my zoo," she called over her shoulder.

"Here, take these." She thrust a spray bottle and a plastic ice cream tub into my hands. Minx tried to squeeze out of the door after us but Izzie picked the Siamese up. "Want another bite, you pest?" she whispered and tossed him gently back inside.

I could hardly wait until we'd closed the shed door. "I know," I said. "I know who Mr Big is." Izzie's reaction wasn't as dramatic as I'd hoped.

"Who?" She was lifted the chameleon out of his tank and placed him on the floor near my foot.

"What are you doing?" I flinched away from him and he rolled his odd-ball eyes at me.

"Giving Karma some exercise. He must be getting so bored. In the summer I take him outside to bask sometimes."

"Don't you want to know who Mr Big is?"

"Yes, of course I do, but I can't think about it at the moment. Quincy's coming here this morning. I've been worrying about it all night. What if he says I'm not looking after my animals properly? What if he wants to take them away?" Then I realized that Izzie was nervous … frightened even.

I backed away as the chameleon did a slow motion walk in my direction.

"You're brilliant at looking after them."

"Aye, but I need to get all these tanks looking perfect. Please help me, Jack. I couldn't stand it if …"

"Tell me what to do," I said.

We cleaned the already clean tanks. Or Izzie did. I handed her the stuff. She put in fresh branches and bits of bark and told me to spray the warm water into the tank.

"On to the leaves," she said. "Chameleons can't drink from a dish. They take moisture from rain or dew."

She made up a breakfast of live grubs and sweet potato — yummy! — for Karma. We put him back in his tank and moved on to Bombina.

Izzie's nervousness was catching and we worked in silence against the clock. It didn't help that we didn't know what time he'd arrive. The sun was shining into the shed and it made the tanks shine and the water drops glitter on the leaves.

Izzie unscrewed the lid of Octavia's tank. I took an automatic step backwards. I still felt nervous around her creatures. The spider was half-hidden under a piece of bark, using it like a cave.

"Hi, sweetie," Izzie said. The tarantula didn't seem bothered when she replaced the water dish and added fresh food. "In the summer, I'll trap you some nice juicy crickets and flies," Izzie promised. She checked the temperature on the thermometer in the shed for the twentieth time, Then she looked around and sighed.

"I can't do any more," she said.

"He'll see how well you look after them. Don't worry." But I was beginning to worry for her. I checked my watch. "Nine thirty. I thought Quincy might have been here by now."

"Izzie? Jack?"

"Quick! Outside! It's mum." Izzie practically pushed me out of the shed and locked the door behind us.

"My word, Izzie, you're getting so secretive about that shed. What have you got in there? Are you hiding something?" Mrs Christie looked at Izzie suspiciously.

"Don't start again, Mum. I said I was sorry about being rude to Sheila. I'll tell her myself if you like."

"Yes, well ... you couldn't have chosen a worse time to upset her as it happens. Lily Fagan, at the Post Office tells me that Magnus is going to sell the land he lets her keep her ponies on. There's no way she'll be able to afford it. Break her heart it will, to let those ponies go."

Izzie sighed, "Oh no. I'll go and see her later."

The brightness of the yellow walls hit me again as we went inside the house and made me blink.

Mr Christie nodded, "Mornin' lad." He was already at the table working on his boats in bulbs. Izzie plonked a kiss on his head as she passed him.

I was desperate to tell Izzie what I'd worked out during the night but she seemed to have forgotten about Mr Big. I thought if I didn't tell her soon I would burst. "Maybe we could eat breakfast on the beach?" I said.

The three of them looked at me as if I was crazy. Then Izzie twigged and said, "Good idea. You've got some of those paper plates left, Mum haven't you?"

Mrs Christie put sausages and a slice of buttered toast on two plates and squirted a circle of ketchup on each. She handed them to us mumbling something about modern youth.

Our feet crunched over the pebbles, as we found

a sheltered hollow in the rocks and settled down with our breakfast. There's something special about eating food on a beach and even the sausages tasted better than normal.

"Are you ready?" I asked triumphantly. "Mr Big … Mr Nasty … The one who's smuggling in live animals, not caring what happens to them, is … Slasher."

Izzie had taken a great bite of her toast but she raised her eyebrows at me. She swallowed. "Don't you think you're getting a wee bit paranoid about this guy?"

"No. Listen. He's here now, right? And the bike rally doesn't start until next month."

"Yeah, but maybe he just wanted a holiday first."

"Maybe. But why is he here, on *this* beach every night?"

"Come on, Jack. I don't think he's after you."

"No. He's not. That's the point." I took a deep breath so that my next words would make a big impact. "He's here on this beach every night because he's waiting for a boat carrying a new load of illegal animals." I licked the ketchup off my fingers.

Izzie was about to take another bite of a sausage so I had the satisfaction of seeing her place it slowly back on the plate in surprise. She looked thoughtful for a minute.

A line of gulls squabbled at the seashore and a wave splashed against the rock sending a fine spray of water towards us. Izzie was still staring at me, her eyes squinting.

"Well?" I wanted a reaction.

"Aaaand ... Slasher asked Sheila if she was the vet and if she would be around if he needed her," Izzie said.

"Yes. I'd forgotten about that. We know this beach is perfect. Remember what Quincy said about it? There's only your house, Sheila's surgery and our bungalow. It's quiet. Hidden away. A boat could easily slip in here with no fuss or noise. We know they must have been here before too, because you and Quincy both said a tarantula couldn't have got far in cold weather."

She suddenly punched my arm. "Do you know, City Boy, I think you're right."

I felt ridiculously happy. "We'll tell Quincy when he comes. It's up to him and your uncle and rest of the police then. Cool, huh? It'd be great if we could help get just one of those criminals arrested."

We finished our breakfast, throwing the scraps to the squawking gulls and watching them fight over them. For the next hour Izzie swung between wanting Quincy to arrive, so we could tell him about Slasher, and not wanting him to arrive in case he didn't approve of her zoo. By midday, I'd taught her to skip stones across the water but there was still no sign of Quincy.

It was getting colder and a thick mist was coming inland. "I'll get my hoodie. We'd better go and see what's keeping him." I said getting up.

"Do you think he'll be in his cave?

"I guess."

Back at Oz Cottage Mum was busy sorting pictures and making notes and just grunted when I said Izzie and I were off for a walk.

Izzie brought the hankies again but this time I knew why. The mist was getting thicker now, rolling in off the sea but stopping, like a wall, just short of the cliffs.

"How are you going to explain Quincy to your parents? They're going to want to know who he is and why he wants to look in your shed." We marched along to keep warm; one two, one two.

"I know. It's only a matter of time before they find out about Octavia. If I can get my dad on his own I'll tell him first. He'll help me when Mum goes into hysterics." She laughed. "A huge hairy tarantula. My poor mum's worst nightmare. She won't even watch spiders on telly."

We followed the path to the cliff top and stood as close to the edge as we dared and I shouted down. The fog was thick on the beach and it was hard to see the entrance to the cave.

"Quincy. Are you there?" My voice echoed out over the sea. We waited but there was no reply.

Izzie tried peering down through the mist. "Quincy?"

The first Bonxie screamed and dropped, mid-flight, right above us. We'd forgotten to pick up the sticks.

Izzie ducked, "Let's go and see if he's in his cave." The steep cliff path led down to a small group of boulders opposite the cave entrance. Inside, it looked deserted. The sleeping bag was unrolled and damp, the camping stove cold.

"Doesn't look like he's been here this morning. Maybe he's still at the Viking Hotel."

"That's too far to walk from here," Izzie said. "What shall we do now?"

I heard it first … a low groan. I spun around s to see where it had come from.

Then Izzie said, "What was that?"

We climbed over the rocks around the cave entrance and saw, what I thought was a bundle of clothes left on the beach. It was difficult to see through the mist, but as we got nearer we heard another groan.

"It's Quincy," I said breaking into a run. He was lying on his side with his leg tucked at a crooked angle under his body. Blood had seeped from a cut on his head and dried in red streaks across his nose and cheek. I moved his face gently and his eyelids fluttered. His skin was grey and felt icy cold when I touched him.

"We need an ambulance," I said in panic. "Get an ambulance. I'll stay with him."

"There's a house just across the way, I'll phone from there." From her voice I could tell that Izzie was as shaken as I was. She raced back across the beach towards the cliff path.

Quincy's leg looked so bent and uncomfortable I thought I should try to move it. But before I could touch him he moaned again and I jumped back

"It's okay. It's me … Jack. We're getting help for you." I felt useless. I couldn't remember any of the First Aid we'd learned at school. I was shivering so much my teeth rattled. I tugged at Quincy's shabby old tramp coat so that it covered him better. Scraps of TV hospital emergencies seeped into my mind … *don't try to move him … keep him warm …*

I ran to the cave and dragged out the sleeping bag. It slithered over the ground behind me with a whooshing noise as I raced back to Quincy's very still body. Wrapping it round him as best I could, I hunkered down on the sand.

The fog now blanked out most of the beach and the shoreline and as I waited, the cries of the invisible birds took on an eerie sound … like children crying in the dark.

Quincy wasn't moving.

"Come on Izzie. Come on Izzie," I whispered over and over.

Something gripped my arm hard and I did my girly scream. It was Quincy, his eyes rolled back but he was trying to focus. "It was … like … Thelwells," he mumbled, then said something else I couldn't understand.

"It's okay. Not long now. The ambulance is coming, Quincy. Don't try to talk."

"No, listen. Tell them … Thelwells. Viking." He gripped my arm harder, trying to stay conscious, but his head slumped to the side and his eyes closed again.

Oh no, I thought. *Don't die. Don't die.* The sound of the siren, at that moment, was the best thing I'd ever heard in my entire life.

Out of the mist, two figures appeared. They were carrying a stretcher and running towards me. Close behind them were policemen; one of whom was Izzie's Uncle Duncan. As soon as they reached me, the paramedics took charge. They dropped to their knees and began to examine Quincy.

Out of the mist, two figures appeared. They

were carrying a stretcher and running towards me. Close behind them were policemen; one of whom was Izzie's Uncle Duncan. As soon as they reached me, the paramedics took charge. They dropped to their knees and began to examine Quincy.

He's alive, son. In a bad way but it looks like we may have got here in time. Well done." One of them patted my shoulder.

"Did you see what happened, Jack?" Izzie's uncle asked.

"No. We found him like this. Where's Izzie?"

"She's in the police car." He pointed to the cliff road above us. "We'll need to ask you both a few questions back at the station."

I was trying to fight back tears of relief. I suddenly felt cold and weak. I just nodded. As they strapped Quincy onto the stretcher I saw his face. Under the blood streaks he was whiter than ever. His eyes were shut tight.

Izzie was in the car looking as shell-shocked as I felt. "Is he …? Is he …?"

"No. He's alive," I whispered. My hands were shaking as I pushed them into my pockets.

The ambulance siren screamed into action and sped away. Izzie turned to look out of the back window. "They'll take him to the Gilbert Bain hospital."

Izzie's uncle got in the driving seat. "I've called your mum and dad, Izzie. They'll meet us at the station." He nodded to me. "They're bringing your mother with them."

Neither of us said a word on the way to the police station. We were both thinking about Quincy and,

I guessed, Izzie was also thinking how to put the best light on hiding a tarantula in her shed.

But to my surprise she suddenly whispered, "Don't tell them about Octavia."

"Are you crazy? This is the police now. We've got to tell them."

"Not, yet. Please, Jack. If Quincy … I mean *when* Quincy comes around he'll persuade my mum to let me keep her."

"No. I …"

"Please, Jack. Please?"

"You kids okay back there?" Izzie's uncle said.

"Yeah."

"Aye."

Izzie was staring me right in the eye, pleading. "Jack?"

"Okay." I sighed. Izzie looked so scared I gave in. "Okay not just yet …"

At the station, Sergeant Duncan Christie — "Call me Duncan," he said — handed us a carton of orange juice each and a Kit-Kat. We sat in the lobby and waited. It was nothing like American films where police stations were always full of people shouting, screaming and being handcuffed.

A single policeman at the desk clicked on his computer. It was very quiet. Just the muffled sound of a passing car now and then. Izzie and I were quiet too.

Through the glass door I saw Mrs Christie arrive, pushing Mr Christie's wheelchair. Mum was with them. They were obviously worried but showed it in different ways. When Mum was upset she went quiet. That didn't apply to Mrs Christie.

We could see her mouth moving even before she even reached us.

"Izabel Christie! What's this all about? You found a body on a beach? What on earth were you doing finding bodies?"

"Muuuum," Izzie rolled her eyes up at the ceiling. "It wasn't a body. We found a man who was hurt. We found him and called the ambulance."

"I'll interview, Jack," Duncan said to Mr Christie. He came round and stood in front of the desk and introduced a young female officer. "This is PC Morna Clarkson. She'll have a chat with you two and Izzie."

They took us down a hall; Mum and I went into one room, Izzie and her parents disappeared into the one next door.

The room was pretty empty; there was table with a tape recorder, four orange chairs and police posters on the wall. Mum patted my hand. "Are you okay, Jack?"

Duncan said, "This is only a formality, Marissa. Jack and Izzie did really well. Probably saved Quincy's life."

"Quincy? Do you know the man then?"

"Yes, he's with the Lothian and Borders police."

Even though Duncan was being so nice, I thought of all the police scenes on the telly where suspects were tricked into confessing and I suddenly felt guilty, even though I hadn't done anything … except help to hide a poisonous spider in a shed.

"Right, Jack in your own time …" Duncan said.

I told him how we had met Quincy and thought he was an animal smuggler. How we had then followed him and found out that he was with the National Wildlife Crime Unit.

"Yep. He's been doing this undercover job on his own time. He's a bit of a fanatic is our Quincy. But he's a good man and cares a lot about the animals." Duncan got up opened the door and called for two coffees. "I don't suppose he was able to tell you what had happened to him?" Duncan asked me.

"No. He was just about unconscious when we got there. He did mumble a few words but they didn't make any sense."

Duncan looked at me closely, "What did he say?"

"Something about a Viking called Thelwell."

Duncan sighed and shook his head. "Doesn't mean a thing to me. It's probably nothing. I'll ask him about it when he comes around."

"Do you want another drink, Jack?" he got up from his chair.

"No thanks. I haven't finished this one yet."

He sat back down again and said, "What I don't understand is, what put the animal smuggling in your mind in the first place?"

I couldn't tell him we'd found a tarantula so I blurted out, "You did. Izzie said you came to the school and gave a talk about it." I could feel my face getting hot and red.

Luckily, at that moment, a policeman knocked the door and came in with a tray of coffee.

I could hear Mrs Christie's high-pitched voice

coming from the room next door and wondered how Izzie was getting on.

Mum on the other hand was very quiet. It was always a warning sign when Mum went quiet.

Another police officer came in and told Duncan that Quincy was still unconscious and his leg was broken in three places but was "as well as could be expected" at the hospital.

"He must have fallen," Duncan said. "Those wretched, dive-bombing Bonxies are enough to push anyone over the edge. It's happened before."

I decided now was a good time to tell Duncan about Slasher. How he was on the beach every night, how Quincy thought our cove was being used to land the animals, and even what Slasher had said to Sheila about needing a vet.

Duncan had been writing down everything I said and I noticed his pen speeding up. He was showing a lot of interest.

"So you see he's a real possibility for Quincy's Mr Big."

"He's on the beach in front of my brother's place every night then?"

"Definitely the last three nights," I said.

"Well, I think that's all I need for now," Duncan said finally. "Jack, why don't you go and see if Izzie's finished?" I didn't wait to be asked again and shot out of the room.

Izzie, Mr and Mrs Christie were in the corridor waiting for us. Mrs Christie was having a real go at Izzie about talking to strange men, I suppose she meant Quincy, and Izzie looked fed-up. As soon as she saw me, Izzie raised her eyebrows and shot me a questioning look. I knew she was asking if I'd told them about Octavia and I shook my head.

Behind me, Mum and Duncan were still talking. I heard Mum say, "Well, I suppose it's a very good cause. My husband was a big supporter of the World Wildlife Fund."

"Thank you, Marissa." Duncan said. "I promise you and Jack will be in no danger. You can go home now. I think we've got everything we need from the kids, if you'll just sign this statement. We'll see you later then?"

Mrs Christie started on Mum as soon as we left the station. "Have they asked you about letting them keep an eye on the beach from your house?" she said. "They seem to have taken what these two told them seriously. Smugglers? Whatever next."

"Yes. I said it would be okay."

Mrs Christie looked surprised, "Really? Well, I won't allow it. I absolutely will not allow it."

"Yes, you will, Denise. You know perfectly well you're just as excited about it as Izzie and me," Mr Christie winked at me and smiled.

Mrs Christie tucked a blanket around his knees. "Well, all right, I suppose ..." she trailed off into a mutter.

8. Slasher

They arrived about eight: Duncan and two other police officers who knocked gently at the door and Mum let them in.

It *was* exciting. Three officers, the uniforms, the feeling of something big about to happen, but I felt jittery too. I went over what I knew about Slasher in my head and still came up with the same idea. Slasher *had* to be the one.

"We'll just sit here in the lad's room, if that's okay? It's got the best view. What time does he usually arrive, Jack?" Duncan was opening a window and there was a sudden rush of cold air and the crash and roll of the waves.

"I don't know. He just seems to be around when I'm going to bed. Is this a stakeout?"

"Yes, I suppose it is," he said.

"Cool." Then I thought, *it won't be so cool if he doesn't turn up. I'm going to look like a complete muppet.*

"Isn't this Maudie Moody's place?" PC Clarkson asked Mum. She was looking around and holding the cross-eyed koala. "Now I understand why it's called Oz Cottage."

"I hear she spends the summers in Australia when it's their winter … so it's not too hot," the other PC said. "Loves surfing they say."

The three of them laughed. "Go on," Duncan said. "She's seventy if she's a day."

It was pretty surreal having three police officers crammed into one small room and Duncan must have thought so too.

"Clarkson and Peters, take the other bedroom. Report any sign of activity."

Mum made coffees and teas and brought them round. She hadn't said much about what had happened at the police station. But I knew she wasn't happy about me following people around, even if they did turn out to be police.

The radio at Duncan's shoulder suddenly crackled. "We're all set Sarge. Over."

"Okay, keep out of sight and remember, don't move until I tell you to. Over."

"We've got three more officers at Izzie's house," he explained to us.

"I don't think Denise was too happy about the idea of hiding police in her house," Mum said.

"She was scared, which is fair enough. I knew big brother Andrew would talk her around, though. Izzie was all for it, too, so she didn't stand a chance."

He took a sip of his coffee and sat on the bed. "My brother was a police sergeant too, you know, before … before his illness. A really good one. He may not have his police legs any more but he's still got his police head. He'll have them in order over there."

We talked about Quincy. "Still no change," Duncan reported. And we talked about smuggling and wildlife in general. Duncan noticed my guitar so we talked about music too. He knew a lot about guitars as well as fiddles. It helped pass the time.

By ten o'clock there was still no sign of Slasher. I was beginning to get a bit bored.

"What if he doesn't come?" I said.

"Then he doesn't come. Even if he does, there could be a completely innocent reason for him being on the beach. It's not against the law. Of course if he *is* involved with the smuggling trade and waiting for a boat, this may not be the right time either. He's been on the beach for three consecutive nights you said?"

I nodded.

"Quincy knew they must be landing somewhere along this stretch but there're a lot of coves here; easy to slide in and out with no one seeing. We'll give it a couple of nights' surveillance and see what happens. These wildlife smugglers are a curse. In it for pure profit. Don't give a hoot about the animals."

I got a drink from the fridge and went into the sitting room where Mum was doing a pretty good impression of watching telly.

It was a mistake. She turned the sound down and said quietly, "So what's all the secrecy about, Jack? Why are you keeping things from me? We used to talk about everything."

I shrugged. I didn't want to get into it with the policemen in the house.

"Strange men in caves?" she continued

I held up my index finger. "One man. One cave."

It wasn't a smart move. Her eyes got *very* bright. Warning sign number two.

"Okay, enough. I'm not having this ..."

I was saved by a shout. “There, Sarge! By that clump of rocks.” The radio crackled at almost the same second and the voice said, “It’s him.”

The other officers joined Duncan. Mum and I tip-toed to the bedroom door and listened from outside the room.

There was tension in the air. I could feel it like electricity. They spoke in whispers. Then Duncan held up his hand. “Shh … listen.”

I heard it too; the low chug, chug, chug, of a boat engine. “Don’t move. Wait until it comes closer to the shore,” Duncan hissed into the radio.

My heart was beating hard and I desperately wanted to see what was happening outside. Mum sensed it and held onto my arm. The waiting was unbearable.

The chug got louder and Duncan suddenly shouted “Go, go, go,” into the radio. The three of them rushed outside with me close behind. I pushed through the prickly bush, ran through the Christie’s garden and onto the beach trying to keep up. Izzie was slightly ahead of me, chasing after her officers.

Mrs Christie was leaning out of her window shouting, “Izabel! Izabel! Izabel!”

A small white boat bobbed on the water. A man was balancing, his legs astride the deck, passing a box to Slasher who was knee-deep in the sea. They heard the commotion and both turned to face the police. The shock on their faces was easy to see even from where I was.

For a second neither of them moved. It was like a snapshot. Then the man on the boat revved the engine, tossed the box into the water and took off out to sea like a rocket … just as the police launch rounded the corner. I wasn't watching the police boat though because to everyone's astonishment Slasher gave a great shout and dived at the box bobbing on the waves. He surfaced, clutching it to his chest like a rugby ball and waded desperately towards the police.

"Help me. Help me. She'll drown."

PC Clarkson was the first to the waterline and, bravely, I thought, she took the box from his outstretched hands.

Izzie was suddenly beside me, "Could be full of tarantulas and scorpions," she said. Her eyes were gleaming.

But Slasher had snatched the box back, placed it carefully on dry land and was on his knees opening it as quickly as he could. Now that it was obvious that he had no intention of making a run for it, the police officers, Izzie and I stood around him in a semi-circle waiting to see what was inside.

He put his hands into the soggy cardboard and pulled out a … kitten; a very wet, white kitten that meowed and hissed and screwed up its face like a little tiger.

"Princess," Slasher sighed and held the tiny creature under his chin.

"Can I just hold her for a minute? I haven't seen her for two weeks. It's this quarantine business. They wanted to lock her up for six months. Six months for a little kitten like this. It's a crime I tell you, a crime."

"Unfortunately for you, sir, it's a crime to bring

an animal into this country without it being quarantined first. Duncan stepped forward. "If you'll just hand over the cat, Sir. We'll take good care of it until this matter is sorted out."

Slasher clutched the damp kitten tightly to his chest, and gave it a kiss on the head, before handing it over to PC Clarkson. "You go with the nice lady, Princess. Daddy will come to see you as soon as he can." Slasher's eyes followed PC Clarkson's every step as she carried up soggy kitten up the beach.

Duncan took hold of Slasher by the arm. "I'm afraid we'll need to talk to you down at the station, sir. It shouldn't take long. We'll arrange for the animal to go into a special cattery or kennels for six months until the officials can confirm it's free from rabies, Mr ... er ...?"

"Pimple," Slasher said. "My name's Harry Pimple."

I heard a splutter of laughter from Izzie and I put my hand over my mouth to stop myself doing the same thing ... too late.

Slasher, or Mr Pimple, heard me and yelled, "Hey kid. I just wanted to tell you I was sorry, yesterday. About getting riled at you on the ferry. I mean, it happens. Kids chuck up, don't they? It's what they do."

"Oh yeah ... thanks." I said through another burst of laughter.

He was barefoot at the edge of the sea and the night took on an even more bizarre feel when the "dangerous" biker inched over the pebbles flinching and swearing at every step as stones stuck in his feet. He reached his black and red boots, sat on a boulder and dragged them on.

Mr Christie was waiting on the patio and the brothers clasped hands as they met. Mum joined us.

"I enjoyed that bit of excitement, Duncan. It felt like the old days there for a while." Izzie's father said. A wide grin spread across his face.

Mrs Christie folded her arms across her chest. "Well I'm glad *you* did, Andrew Christie, because it frightened the life out of me. That daughter of yours is getting out of hand, too. Running outside with the officers like that."

"Ach, put the kettle on, Denise, and stop fussing," her husband told her with a smile. He turned to me, "We call her 'Tammie Norie,' don't we, Izzie?" He nodded towards his wife.

"That's what you call the puffins, isn't it?" I asked.

"Yes, and she's always huffin' and puffin' about something," he grinned. Mrs Christie tutted but she didn't look upset.

Harry Pimple was taken off in the police car. "I reckon the five of them can manage a hardened criminal like that," Duncan said. "He can come back later for his bike."

We stayed at the Christie's house for a while. Mrs Christie brought out a chocolate cake.

"You must have a magic cupboard," Mum said. "How do you do manage to cook all this wonderful food?"

I could see Mrs Christie was pleased and gave Mum the biggest slice.

"Harry Pimple?" Izzie kept saying. "I reckon I'd call myself Slasher, too, if I was called Harry Pimple."

"Could've been worse. He could have been called Ivor."

"Ivor Pimple," Izzie shrieked. "Ivor Pimple."

I was chuffed with my joke and repeated it several times over the next hour, until Izzie stopped laughing and said, "Okay ... not funny any more."

Before I got into bed that night I looked out on a "Slasher-less" beach. In a weird way, I kind of missed him.

"I hate them."

Izzie was in a really bad mood the next morning.

"I usually get out of going to these things. I mean do I *look* like I'd enjoy a Glitz and Glam party?"

With her torn jeans, dirty trainers and hair dragged back into a ponytail with a shoelace, I had to admit, that no she didn't.

"Spray Karma, will you, Jack? This friend at school is having it and I was invited ages ago, but I thought I'd got out of going. Dad says I should go to keep Mum happy. Mum thinks I should do some *normal* girls' stuff, though I'm not sure what she means by that."

I tried my Ivor Pimple joke again but it wasn't the time. She just gave me an irritated look. I gave up.

I grabbed the bottle of warm water and lifted the lid of Karma's tank. As I watched, he changed from a brownish grey colour to a bright blue and green.

"Wow ..." I said.

Izzie looked over my shoulder, "He likes you," she said. "That's his happy colour."

"Really? Well I like you too, Karma, old mate." The chameleon's long thin tongue snaked out and snatched a mealie worm from the other side of the tank. "But you still freak me out," I whispered.

Bombina the Fire Bellied Toad was definitely my favourite, not just because of his colours, but because he always seemed so happy; hopping around or swimming. I loved his squeaky-toy noises too. But I noticed something that didn't seem right.

"Izzie? Look at Bombina."

She was beside me in a flash. Then she smiled. "This is really cool. Watch this." Bombina sat quite still, coughing and bloating up like he was going to explode.

"Is he dying?"

"He's shedding," Izzie said. As we watched he began ripping his skin off with his mouth and eating it.

"Ugh," I said. "Gross!"

"It's full of *toady* goodness."

It took a while but he looked better in his new skin, fresher and brighter. He hopped into the water with one of his squeaks and swam to the bottom of his tank.

"Show over," Izzie said.

"Heard any more about Slasher?" I asked her.

Izzie shrugged. "He'll get a fine, the kitten will go into quarantine, then after six months he can collect his Princess and take her home."

"It was so cool when all that was happening though, wasn't it."

"Aye, cool."

I tried my Ivor Pimple joke again but she just rolled her eyes.

"What time are you going?" I asked.

"About eleven, but I'll be back this evening. We're having lunch at the Happy Haddock, that'll be good, and then back to Emma's for this glam thing. A woman is coming to make us up and do our hair."

Izzie sounded so miserable you'd have thought she was going to a hospital instead of a party. I tried to look sorry for her.

After she'd left, I mooched around the house and generally got under Mum's feet. "Izzie's gone to a Glitz and Glam party," I told her.

Mum pursed her lips. "Wouldn't have thought that was Izzie's thing," she said.

"It really isn't."

We were still a bit awkward together and weren't talking much. I realized Mum was hurt because I'd been keeping things from her but I couldn't put that right now. I hadn't played my guitar in days. I took it out, strummed a few chords and put it back in its case again. I was bored.

Mrs Christie came round. "Thought you might like to know, Jack, that Duncan called and the man you and Izzie found on the beach has come out of his coma. He's still drifting in and out of consciousness but he's better than he was. He doesn't remember a thing about the accident though. It's completely gone from his mind.

I was glad Quincy was going to be okay, but I felt guilty that I hadn't thought about him more. All the excitement with Slasher had taken over and pushed him to the back of my mind.

Mum decided to get some shots of the great stones on top of the hill so I watched telly and tried to guess what the stuff going up for auction would fetch. I was *really* bored. So bored that when Sheila came to ask if I'd help her muck out the ponies, I said "Yes."

"I gave Izzie a shout but Denise says she gone to a Glitz and Glam party. I bet she had to be bribed to do that!" She grinned.

I knew what to expect with the mucking out this time, but the ponies more than made up for the stink and the work. I was trying to remember their names. "That one's easy. He's Nuggle; you named him after a local sea creature or something."

Nuggle was in front, as always, and pushing at my hand for his mint. The others crowded round and he gave two short sharp kicks of his back legs to keep them away.

"He's a pain but I think I like him best." I said, reaching out to give him a pat on the neck.

"I know what you mean. I love them all but he's such an attention-seeker that he stands out from the crowd every time."

"That one is Kilty. I can't remember that one's name …"

"Conner," Sheila said. "And that one, the one with the lovely eyes?"

"Amber," I said, pleased with myself for remembering.

We went into the stable and Sheila shut the bottom half of the barn door to keep them outside while we worked. We soon cleared the manure and started filling the wheelbarrow with the wet straw.

Sheila had given me a different pair of gloves this time and they fitted, but the boots were still too small and hurt my feet. It wasn't the same without Izzie. I didn't know what to talk to Sheila about. "Exciting all that on the beach last night wasn't it?"

"What do you mean? I was out on a call last night."

"The police ambush and Slasher."

She stopped forking the straw and leaned on the handle of her fork. She was frowning at me, looking almost angry. "What police ambush? Who's Slasher?"

I told her about Duncan and the other police officers hiding at the house and what had happened with Slasher and the kitten. I tried to make it amusing but she didn't laugh so I tried my Ivor Pimple joke … but she didn't laugh at that either.

"So who filled your head with all this wildlife smuggling nonsense?"

"It's not nonsense. Quincy, the man we found injured on the beach, he's with the …" I hesitated wanting to get the full title right, " … he's with the National Wildlife Crime Unit. It's part of the Lothian and Borders Police Force.

"So I understand. I heard about you and Izzie finding him. Must have been a shock."

"It was. We thought he was dead."

Sheila was banking the straw around the edges of the stable and tucking it in to make a neat edge. "Put a bit more over there, Jack. So what did he say when you found him?"

"Not much, he passed out. He mumbled something that didn't make sense."

She'd turned to face me again. "What exactly did he mumble?"

"Something about a Viking and a name I can't remember now."

"Well most of us here on Shetland are descended from the Vikings. How is he now?"

I shrugged and kept forking the straw. "His leg's a mess, so he'll be in hospital for a while. He doesn't remember anything about the accident. He remembers walking up the cliff path and then waking up in hospital the next day."

"If you'll just empty the wheelbarrow onto the manure pile, that's us finished. Thanks for your help, Jack."

"S'okay."

The ponies nudged and bumped at us as soon as we were outside. Sheila handed me half a pack of mints. I could see why she loved them so much. Nuggle even followed me to the muck heap and back. When I'd given away my last mint he bit my sleeve and tugged and tugged with his big yellow teeth. Sheila had to pull him off me.

We were walking back to the house when I said, "I'm sorry you're losing the field. What are you going to do with the ponies? Mrs Christie said the farmer wants to sell this field and you'll have nowhere to keep them."

"Oh, that's all taken care of. I'm going to buy it off him. I've made an offer for another six acres too. I'll be able to take more ponies. Now … I've got some Jaffa cakes in the house. Do you reckon we could finish them off without Izzie's help?"

"I'll give it my best shot." The weather had changed again and the drizzle was now heavy rain. We made a run for it.

Her lounge was warm with fat, comfy chairs everywhere. Sheila tipped a pile of magazines off one and said, "Make yourself at home." I was feeling tired after the excitement of the night before and then the mucking out, and was just nodding off when a frantic banging at the door behind me made me jump to my feet. I turned and saw someone peering though the glass. A crazy man, with hair sleeked down by the rain and his face screwed up with rage, was pulling at the patio doors. They must have been locked and he banged with his fist again.

9. Penelope rides again

"They've called it off," he shouted. "They've called it off. They said it's too dangerous here now. Let me in."

Sheila rushed into the room with a tray and froze. She jerked her head in my direction, to let the man know I was there. At the same time, I realized it was Louis, the waiter from the Viking Hotel, who was hammering at the door.

When he saw me, Louis calmed down immediately. Sheila put the tray on the coffee table, unlocked the doors and threw them open. "As you can see Louis, I have a guest. Let's talk outside, shall we?"

"Here, Jack, have a read or something. I won't be long." She grabbed the nearest book and handed it to me. It was a book of cartoons called *Penelope rides again*, with pictures of funny little girls riding Shetland ponies.

I saw Sheila grab Louis's sleeve, and although he was almost twice her size, she virtually dragged him down the path to the door of his caravan. There was an argument about something. They didn't seem to notice how wet they were getting in the rain.

Louis went into the caravan, slamming the door so hard the little caravan shook and Sheila started back up the path to the house. I didn't want her to know I'd been watching so I pretended I was reading the book. The cartoons were familiar; I must have seen them somewhere before. As I turned the pages, something caught my eye. The man who'd drawn the pony cartoons was called "Thelwell." *That* was the name Quincy had said on the beach. Thelwell.

"Sorry about that," Sheila said. She picked up a towel that was drying on the radiator and began rubbing her hair. "Louis has problems with that dog of his; nothing to worry about."

But she did seem worried and I wondered what had happened to make Louis so angry and cause an argument between them.

"Here are the Jaffa cakes I promised." She handed me the plate but didn't look at me. She was miles away. The rain rattled the windows outside but we were silent. All you could hear was me sipping at a cup of hot chocolate and the rustle of paper when I took another biscuit. It was getting embarrassing, so for something to say I blurted out. "We found a tarantula."

The change in Sheila was startling. She stared right at me and her eyes grew wide, she spoke very slowly, "What did you just say?" Her skin looked white against her red hair.

She was making me feel guilty. Like I'd just confessed to something terrible.

"I said ... Izzie and I found a tarantula." Sheila kept staring at me with her mouth open. "By the fridge," I added, "Izzie's got it in her zoo. It's a Mexican red-kneed spider."

"It's still alive?" Sheila spoke at last. "So that's why Izzie was so upset about me going into her shed the other night. She didn't want me to see the spider. I knew there was something odd going on."

I nodded. "She doesn't want anyone to know about it."

"Who else have you told, Jack?"

"No one, it's a secret. Izzie's afraid they'll take it away from her."

"She's right," Sheila was getting up out of her chair. "Do you understand? She's absolutely right. If anyone finds out about the tarantula it will be taken away and destroyed. Make sure you tell Izzie that. We wouldn't want it killed would we?"

She said it so fiercely that I shook my head and decided not to tell her that Quincy knew about it as well.

"Time you were off, lad. I've patients to see."

"But I haven't finished my ..."

"I'll take that." She snatched my half-full mug of chocolate away from me and put it on the sideboard." You'd better be going. Your mother will wonder where you are. Here ... take these with you."

She pushed the Jaffa cakes into my hand. As we passed the coats in the hall she grabbed my hoodie and thrust that at me too. Before I knew what was happening I was out of the door and standing in the rain holding my coat and a packet of biscuits.

It had been a weird day. I wished Izzie was back. I wondered how she was getting on at her party.

I was watching out of the window when Mrs Christie's Fiat van returned from picking Izzie up. I was out of the door and standing by the passenger seat almost before they stopped. When she got out, Izzie looked me straight in the eye and said "Don't say anything."

I put my finger and thumb together and drew them across my lips like a zip. I didn't speak but I knew my face showed what I was thinking. Izzie looked terrible: her hair was coloured in streaks of blue and red and pinned up in some sort of weird hairstyle; her eyes were ringed with purple and surrounded with thick black eyelashes like twin spiders; she even had lipstick on.

"Doesn't she look grown up?" Mrs Christie patted Izzie's hair.

"I ..."

"No. Not a word," Izzie raised both hands to stop me answering her mother and I saw every fingernail was painted a different colour ... they looked like Smarties.

"I'm going inside for a shower. I'll see you after," she said.

I slouched back inside Oz Cottage and had a micro-waved veggie burger with Mum. When Izzie knocked later she was back to normal. Neither of us mentioned the Glitz and Glam face.

She spoke to Mum first. "Marissa, Mum wants to know if you and Jack want to come to the Gilbert Bain Hospital to visit Quincy with us this evening? We can be ready at six."

Mum glanced at me and I nodded. We didn't have time to get flowers or chocolate so Mum dropped a few of her photo printouts into an envelope and off we went. It was still raining and the windows of Mrs Christie's van were misted up.

Izzie and I played noughts and crosses on the rear windscreen.

"He's only got a mother in Cornwall and a sister in Canada, Duncan says. Poor man. I've made him some of my shortbread." Mrs Christie was telling Mum.

"Is he conscious now then?"

"Still a bit woozy apparently. He had surgery on his leg yesterday. It was a lucky escape. If it wasn't for Izzie and Jack … well, heaven knows what might have happened." Mrs Christie had done a complete turnaround and now thought we were heroes. Especially after the local radio station, SIBC, had called her and asked if we'd do an interview. Neither of us wanted to, but I had a feeling Mrs Christie would do it for us.

We arrived at the Gilbert Bain hospital Mrs Christie called, "yoo hoo" to the receptionist and asked for Quincy Barr. "They know me in here," she said. "We come so often for Andrew's check-ups." The girl typed into her computer and gave us directions.

Quincy was propped up on several pillows with a white sheet pulled up to his chest. He looked like ghost. The gash on his head was stitched with black thread and looked raw and painful. Because the cut was just over his mole, it had the odd effect of looking like a third eye. A single "Get Well Soon" card stood on his locker beside a box of unopened After Eight Mints.

He was asleep but that didn't bother Mrs Christie, "Mr Barr, Mr Barr, I've brought you some shortbread." She rattled the tin near his ear.

"Maybe we should just let him rest and come back tomorrow?" Mum said.

I took a peep inside his card. It said, *"Good luck, Quincy, from your pals at Lerwick Police station."*

Mrs Christie was still rattling her tin like the charity collectors you see outside supermarkets. "But, I'm sure Mr Barr would want to say thank you to the children who saved his life."

Mum and I were embarrassed and Izzie looked like she wanted the floor to swallow her up.

"Is he a detective or a constable or …"

"Muuum … shhh, he's sleeping."

Quincy's eyes fluttered open.

"Ah, there you are, Mr Barr. We've brought the children to see you."

Quincy was confused. He looked from Mrs Christie to Izzie and then to Mum and me. I could see he didn't remember us. Then something registered.

"Are you the kids who found me on the beach?" His voice sounded dry, like he had a sore throat. I wondered if it hurt him to talk.

I nodded.

"I hear I owe you both a big thank you."

"That's okay," Izzie said. Quincy's eyelids fluttered again. He seemed to be having trouble keeping his eyes open.

Mum put the envelope with the photos on Quincy's locker. "I really think we should go and let Mr Barr have a sleep."

"Please forgive me, Mrs … um?" Quincy struggled awake again.

I introduced Mum and Mrs Christie, who took the opportunity to push the tin of shortbread under his nose again. “Freshly cooked this morning,” she said.

He thanked her, took it and reached across to put it on his locker. The sheet drew back and I saw his leg. It was puffy and stained yellow-brown with dye. There was a metal rod skewering it like a kebab. I felt suddenly dizzy and caught hold of the edge of the bed.

Izzie moved in closer. “That’s amazing. They’ve fixed your leg back together again with metal bolts and screws.” She was obviously impressed. I shouldn’t have been surprised. What else could I have expected from a girl who loved poisonous toads and venomous spiders.

“Thank you, all of you, so much for coming. You must excuse me if I drift off. I had the surgery yesterday and I still feel a bit …”

A nurse came in and said, “I think that’s long enough, everyone. Mr Barr is still recovering from his operation. Perhaps tomorrow …”

I was relieved and I guess Quincy was too. He was asleep before we were out of the door.

We parked down near the boats. The rain stopped and although the streets were shiny wet, it wasn’t cold. We bought jacket potatoes from a takeaway and headed for the harbour. Mum and Mrs Christie were ahead, swapping baby stories. We trailed behind.

“Doesn’t your dad mind being left on his own?”

“You’re kidding. He gave me the twenty pounds to buy food and keep Mum out as long as possible. He wants to get on with writing his craft articles for the magazines.”

We'd reached the square called Market Cross and Izzie said, "See there, on that wall. It's a webcam." We ran passed a big old-fashioned lamp in the middle of the road and stood outside a solicitor's office waving and making stupid faces at the camera.

"Do you think anyone is watching?"

Izzie shrugged. "Who cares."

The harbour was busy with people getting on and off boats, lorries being loaded and unloaded, and boats of all sizes and colours. Over all the activity drifted the chug and smell of engines and the cries of gulls.

At first, it looked like a tangle of ropes and masts as far as you could see but when we came closer I saw that the boats were neatly moored in lines. Some of them had rubber tyres cut into halves, tied to the sides. I guessed that was to stop any damage if they banged together in the wind.

Izzie waved and said hello to some people. One fisherman stopped to ask how her dad was getting on. "Good man, your father," he said. "One of the best."

"I know." Izzie said. She was smiling.

When we caught up with our mothers, Mum was taking photographs of a round building covered in squares of bright pictures made from bits of pottery.

"Our mosaic pumping station," Mrs Christie said proudly.

It was colder nearer the sea and I put my hood up and my hands in my pockets. Izzie did the same. I made sure we couldn't be overheard.

"It's hard to believe we thought poor Quincy was a smuggler, isn't it?"

"Yes. Did you see what they'd done to his leg? Amazing. Must hurt like crazy though."

I didn't want to think about Quincy's leg. "Then, we were sure Slasher was a criminal and we were wrong again. Slasher wasn't Mr Big; just Mr Big Softie. Didn't do too well as detectives, did we?"

The bright orange of the local lifeboat came into view and Mum turned her attention to it and clicked away. The wind was picking up; ropes and sails vibrated and boats rocked in their moorings.

"I'd love to find out who sneaked Octavia in," Izzie said. "You can bet she wasn't the only spider. Who knows how many tarantulas died that night, either dropped or thrown into the sea to drift away on the tide."

It was a horrible picture; spiders drowning, struggling for life in the cold dark water. "I'd have liked to have done something to catch them," I said. "But it's too late now. I don't suppose they'll come into our cove again." I was thinking of it as *our* cove now. "They'll have been frightened off by the police last night."

"Aye, so there's no point in keeping watch anymore."

"It *was* cool last night though, wasn't it, running out with the police and everything?"

She smiled. "It was cool, alright."

Mum and Mrs Christie were heading back towards us. I heard Mum laughing. It wasn't something I'd heard much over the last few days.

The wind blew my fringe across my eyes. I brushed it aside.

"Quincy didn't remember us, did he? Do you think he'll get his memory back?"

"Dunno," Izzie said. "I hope so."

Back at Oz Cottage Mum clicked through the camera viewer. "This place is just amazing. I've taken more good shots in the time we've been here than I have for years. Everywhere you look there's something interesting to photograph. I reckon I could come back year after year and still find something different."

"I wouldn't mind coming back again."

Mum shot me a surprised look. "Really?"

I turned on the telly and didn't answer.

I was nodding off on the leather sofa so I got up and went into my room. Mum had already gone to bed. I tried a few chords on my guitar but wasn't in the mood. I changed for bed, climbed under the duvet and plugged my iPod into my ears.

I was asleep when a frantic knocking at my window woke me up. For a minute, before I was properly awake, I thought it was Louis banging like he'd done on Sheila's door earlier. It started again, louder than before. I jumped out of bed and tugged up one corner of the curtain. It was Izzie. Her face wet with rain and tears.

I opened my window. Immediately the wind rushed into the room like a cold river. I shivered.

"Jack, Jack … she's gone."

"What? Who?"

"Octavia's gone."

Horrified, I did a quick check of my room. I

don't know what I was thinking. As if she'd return to where we found her like some homing pigeon. "How did she get out?"

"*She* didn't," Izzie was crying openly now. "Her tank has gone too. Someone stole her. I was looking for Minx in the garden. I could hear him wailing and it was coming from the shed. He must have got in when the thief did. Whoever it was must have found the key under the stone and now she's gone."

Even I realized this wasn't the time to say, "I told you the key wouldn't be safe there."

"Oh, Jack what are we going to do?"

She was shivering like mad and her hair was dripping wet.

"Let me think." I rubbed at my eyes top get rid of the last bit of sleepiness. "You'd better come in. Go around to the door."

I was whispering but Izzie's voice was getting louder as she grew more upset. "I can't come in. Mum and Dad think I'm still looking for Minx."

"Jack? Are you okay?" Mum called from her room.

"Yes, yes I'm just … um … singing."

I turned back to speak to Izzie but she had gone.

10. Octavia

I didn't know what to do. Should I have got dressed and gone out after her? No, she'd have been back inside her house by now. I'd have to wait until morning. I paced up and down my room and when that did nothing to make me feel better, I went into the lounge and stared up at the standing stones on the hill. They didn't give me any ideas to help me sort out the problem. One thing I was sure of; we couldn't go to the police. But who could have stolen Octavia? Come to that, who would have wanted to?

In the end I gave up and went to bed. I couldn't think of a likely thief. I slept badly that night and had mixed-up dreams. Twice I woke up shouting, convinced that Octavia was in my bed, crawling up my leg.

"I've been awake all night. I just can't think who could have taken her and why?" Izzie said for the tenth time. She looked worse that I felt. She'd obviously been crying for hours; her eyes were red and her face seemed smaller somehow.

Karma was doing his slow goose-step on the shed floor. His twiggy feet made scratching noises on the wood, and I still didn't trust him not to make a sudden dash and run up my trouser leg. On the shelf was a gaping space where Octavia should have been. We'd searched the shed three times, stupidly hoping that maybe the tarantula had gone walkabout, carrying her tank on her back

"Besides no one knew she was here except you and me … oh, and Quincy, but the poor man doesn't remember a thing."

She'd said that a few times too. It was no good. I couldn't put it off any longer. I decided to come clean.

I took a deep breath. "And Sheila," I said.

"Sheila?"

"I told her yesterday."

Izzie looked angry for a minute and then sighed. "Well I guess that's okay. I trust Sheila. What did she say when you told her?"

"That we should keep it a secret or someone might take her away … or even kill her."

"Well there you are then, Sheila agrees with us. She wouldn't tell anyone."

I could see that Izzie was about to cry again. "We've got to finish cleaning Karma and Bombina," I said. "We can't neglect them just because Octavia is missing."

"You're right," she said, sniffing and wiping her nose with the back of her hand.

We spent the next half hour feeding, cleaning and replacing water, but I knew Izzie's heart wasn't in it. She worked slowly, without her usual energy. I realized she was probably thinking the worst; that Octavia was already dead. If I was honest with myself it was what I was thinking too.

We would be going home tomorrow evening on the seven o'clock ferry. Before I left Shetland, I wanted more than anything to get Octavia back for Izzie, to make her happy again. But I didn't have a clue where to look or what to do.

Mum made cheese sandwiches for lunch but I wasn't very hungry and Izzie ate nothing at all. "My, we've got a gloomy pair here today. What's up?"

We made an effort at normal conversation. We talked about Mum's photos, and about the whale, but it was something Mum said that got me thinking. We were talking about Sheila and her Shetland ponies. Izzie was surprised to hear that Sheila was buying the land.

"That's great news. I thought she was broke but she's obviously found the money from somewhere."

Mum took another sandwich and offered the plate to Izzie and then to me. "I was thinking Sheila that could give rides on those little ponies of hers if she needs extra cash. There're plenty of people here in the summer and I bet lots of little girls would be queuing up to ride on those cute Shetland ponies."

It was the little girls on ponies that did it. Things began to click in my mind. They didn't make complete sense but some of them slotted together like Tetris blocks. The cartoon book that Sheila had given me to read — the one called *Penelope rides again* — was written by a cartoonist named Thelwell. I remembered now where I'd seen the cartoons before ... on Sheila's van.

The ponies that Mr Christie had painted onto Sheila's white van were identical to the ones in the book. How could I have been so stupid? And what if ... what if when Quincy said "Thelwell," he'd meant the cartoons? He might have meant that he'd seen the van. My heart began beating with excitement. So, if Quincy meant Sheila's van, what had he been trying to tell me about it?

Mum nudged me out of my daydream and said, "Jack, it's getting cold again. Izzie wants to look at my pictures — are you coming in?"

"Um, no, I think I'll go for a walk along the beach. It might be my last chance before we leave."

"Okay."

I left them to the photographs and headed to the cove. The tide was coming in but I could see by the line of seaweed that it had quite a way to come yet, so I'd be safe. I needed to think clearly. I breathed in the cold salty air.

When would Quincy have seen the van? That morning? No, the ambulance man said he'd been there all night so it must have been the night before. Why would Sheila have been down near Quincy's cave?

I took my shoes and socks off to paddle in the water. I rolled up my jeans. I thought a stroll along the water's edge might help me make sense of things. I didn't expect it to be quite so cold. The water was freezing and took my breath away. I saw a blob floating just off the pebbles of the sea floor. I thought it was a plastic bag until I got closer and saw tentacles. A wave washed the jellyfish towards me and I ran.

But, Sheila didn't drive the van much. Izzie had said she cycled everywhere. Louis, on the other hand, drove the van quite a lot. Another Tetris brick slotted into place. Maybe Quincy told Louis about the tarantula. *But even if he did why would Louis have taken the tarantula?*

Quincy's voice came into my head and I clearly heard him say. *"It's not just a pet anymore, Izzie. It's evidence."* That's what he'd told us when we were in the cave.

My feet hurt stumbling over the rocks and pebbles, and a piece of seaweed was trapped between my toes. I wiped them on the bottom of my T-shirt and put my socks and shoes back on, my feet still grainy with sand.

So maybe, just maybe, Louis was the smuggler. He lived in the cove. The caravan was out of sight and close to the water; perfect for night time smuggling. It would be a good reason to keep a ferocious dog, to stop people snooping around. There was another click in my mind. *When I found Quincy he'd also said "Viking." Louis worked at the Viking perhaps that's what Quincy had been trying to tell me? Suddenly, Louis as the wildlife smuggler was making more and more sense. So Louis taking Octavia made the most sense of all; he lived close to Izzie's shed too. It would have been easy for him to have sneaked into the garden, forced the padlock on the shed door and made off with the tarantula. I had no proof of anything. But we could always check that caravan of his.*

On my way back across the beach I noticed a strange bird. It was huge, orange and blue and hovered, with an odd jerking movement, just over a line of rocks. I could see the beak and claws. I'd never seen anything like it before in any book or on telly. I forgot about Louis and even Octavia for a minute, as I watched, fascinated, and tried to take in every detail so that I could ask Izzie what it was. It made a sudden swoop downwards and disappeared behind a large boulder. I climbed up to get a better look. I saw a father and son pull the bird to the ground, flatten it and roll it up. Only then did I realize it was a child's kite.

I made my way back to Oz Cottage trying to persuade myself that I had known it was a kite all along.

I wasn't sure what to tell Izzie. If I was right, then the terrible truth was that Louis might have killed Octavia to get rid of the evidence. But, if he hadn't done it yet, there was still a chance we could get her back.

Mum and Izzie had finished looking at pictures and were talking about the cameras.

"It's my birthday next month and mum and dad are going to get me a digital." Izzie's mood had affected Mum and conversation between them was awkward so I told them my kid's kite story and that helped, bringing their smiles back, if only for a while.

"I was thinking of popping into town to get some bits and pieces. Do you two want to come?" Mum said.

"Um … no we'll go over to Izzie's house."

It took ages for Mum to make a list, get her coat on and find the car keys she'd lost, but at last the red Clio disappeared around the bend of the road.

As soon as she was out of sight, I told Izzie

what I thought about the cartoons on the van and Louis working at the Viking. She didn't seem very enthusiastic.

"It's all a bit ... what's the word they use in detective programmes? Circum ... circum ... stantial? That's it, circumstantial."

"Doesn't that just mean they can't prove it? We could prove it."

"How?"

"We could search his caravan."

Izzie seemed tired of the whole thing and I suddenly realized just how badly Octavia's disappearance had affected her. "How would he have known that I even had a tarantula?" she asked.

"I dunno. He might have heard me telling Sheila. He lives close enough and he'd been banging at the door."

Izzie shook her head "The way we're going, Jack, we'll have accused everyone on the island of being a smuggler. We can't go breaking into someone's home, anyway."

"Not even if he has Octavia in there?

"I'm not stupid. If Louis *is* the criminal he'll have killed Octavia by now to get rid of the evidence." Her eyes filled with tears and she turned away so that I wouldn't see her cry. I tried a different approach.

"We can't just give up on her. What if she's still alive? She survived being captured and shipped to a cold country. She survived whatever happened to the other tarantulas that night, too. She managed to crawl to safety against all the odds. Octavia is a survivor."

That worked. Izzie straightened up and turned around to face me.

"You're right. We've got to try." The light was back is Izzie's silver eyes and I was glad to see it.

Louis's caravan was nearer the shore than Sheila's house, surrounded by a bramble hedge and closed off by a rusty old cattle gate.

"He's probably working at the hotel," Izzie said. Around the corner from the hedge was the pathway that led straight up to Sheila's house and her patio doors. "I'd tell Sheila but I know she's not in. I saw her cycle down the road when I was with your mum."

"We've got nothing to tell her yet anyway. It'll sound like a load of rubbish. We have to get some proof to back up what we think. So, are you ready?"

Izzie nodded.

I gripped the gate and was about to swing my leg over, when there was a roar that ripped through the afternoon and sent a group of gulls squawking into the air. A huge Rottweiler threw himself, with full force, against the gate. We'd forgotten about King. We both screamed and leapt back as his great jaws fastened on the cross bar. Flecks of saliva scattered in all directions from his great jaws. I could see he was chained but I wasn't going to hang around to see how far the chain stretched. Izzie had had the same idea and we bolted as far down the track as we could.

We were both scared and shaking and for no reason at all burst into helpless laughter.

"It's not funny," Izzie said, giggling uncontrollably.

"I know, I know. He frightened me to death," I howled until my sides hurt and I had to lean over to catch my breath. Our laughter provoked King even more and he snarled and growled and savaged the metal gate with fury.

When we at last controlled ourselves, I said, "That's the end of that then. We can't go sneaking around Louis's caravan or we'll be eaten alive by King."

Izzie was hiccupping after her laughing fit. "We could distract him ... hic."

"How? Shall I try my juggling act?"

"Hic ... Meat," she said.

Mrs Christie gave Izzie a glass of water for her hiccups and told her to drink it from the other side of the glass. This ended with a wet, annoyed Izzie and a very amused Mr Christie.

"Blow on your thumb, Izzie, that's what my father always told us to do." His eyes crinkled with mischief under his bushy eyebrows.

"My mum said her parents used to make her say pineapple over and over again," I chipped in.

Ten minutes later Izzie was still hiccupping. "I'll never be able to sneak out any food with mum and dad there. Let's go to your place ... hic."

Our 'biggest fridge in the world' fridge wasn't much help. "Mum doesn't eat a lot of meat."

We rummaged through brown rice, wholemeal bread and some odd looking mushrooms in a plastic bag. But, tucked away in the back of the freezer, was a packet of my favourite chicken nuggets.

"What do you think?"

"Worth a try ... hic." Izzie said.

It seemed like a good plan until we got back to the caravan. King's snarling and lunging at the gate made the hair on the back of my neck prickle.

"Right the plan is ... um ..." Thinking on my feet I said. "You throw the nuggets over the gate as far as you can. Keep him on the other side away from the caravan. I'll get in and look through the window." I sounded a lot braver than I felt.

Izzie hurled the first frozen chicken nugget through the air. King took off like a greyhound, found it in the grass and gobbled it up.

"He loves them ... hic ... Quick, get over the gate. Go on."

Another nugget flew past my left shoulder. I wanted to get this over with as quickly as possible and while King rummaged among the brambles, I vaulted over the gate and ran to the nearest caravan window. My heart was beating like crazy; thumping nearly out of my chest.

Another nugget whizzed past. The glass was so dirty it was hard to see inside. I rubbed a patch clean with my T-shirt and peered in. When my eyes got used to the gloom, I saw clothes scattered everywhere and stuff piled on top of shelves and cupboards, and, there on the draining board by the sink, sat the tarantula in her tank.

I desperately wanted to shout to Izzie but was afraid of attracting the mad dog. The chicken nuggets were flying fast now and it didn't take a genius to work out that there couldn't have been many left.

I had to act quickly. I grabbed the caravan door and it opened. I didn't let myself think about what I was doing. There wasn't time. I almost fell over several pairs of shoes on the floor but I made it to the tank and, with shaking hands, lifted it up and rushed back outside.

"Quick … hic … Quick. Jack!" I'm down to the last piece!" Izzie was panicking but not as much as I was. Never, in my worst nightmare had I ever imagined that I'd be running from a savage dog while carrying a venomous spider.

How I managed to get over the gate carrying the glass tank I'll never know. But I did. I heard King snarling and growling just behind me.

"You've got her. You've got her. Thank you *sooo* much." Izzie was crying again but with happiness this time. She cuddled the tank as if it was a teddy bear. Octavia looked a bit rattled after the activity but she wasn't hurt. "I've never been so scared. I thought any minute that dog would get you and savage you to death."

The same thought had flashed through my mind too. "It cured your hiccups anyway," I said.

We heard a loud bark and King stood watching us from the other side of the gate. He wasn't growling and flashing his teeth; he was whimpering and wagging his tail. Izzie put the tank with Octavia carefully on the grass and walked over to him. She pulled the soggy bag of nuggets from her pocket and took out the last one, passing it slowly through the bars of the gate. King accepted it gently, licking her hand as he did.

"You old fraud," she laughed.

We heard an engine and Sheila's pony van bumped along the lane towards her house.

"He's back." Izzie snatched up the tank and we escaped over the small hill, down onto the beach out of sight of the caravan.

Maybe Octavia was glad to be back in the Izzie-zoo, it was hard to tell. Izzie was certainly glad to have her there. She made cooing noises at the squatting spider though the glass.

I was nervous and glanced over my shoulder at the shed door several times. What Izzie and I hadn't thought about yet was what would happen now. Louis was home from work and it wouldn't take him long to notice that the tarantula had gone. It wouldn't take too long for him to figure out who had taken her either.

"Izzie, we've got to tell Sheila," I said. "She'll stop Louis trying to get her back again. Maybe she can tell the police without mentioning Octavia."

"Get her back again?"

"I know he seems a nice enough guy, but now we know he's a thief and probably Quincy's Mr Big, he might get desperate and ..."

"Stop it, Jack. You're scaring me."

I was scaring myself, and when the next thought popped into my head, I scared myself even more. "What if ...?" I said. "What if Quincy didn't fall off the cliff? What if Louis pushed him?"

Izzie looked at me in alarm "We've got to tell Sheila. She'll help us."

Sheila's bike was propped against the hedge and we saw her in the field with the ponies. Even from a distance it was clear how much she loved them.

They gathered around her like children while she stroked and petted them, sometimes rubbing her face against theirs.

She saw us at the gate, waved and headed across the field towards us. "Hello, you two. How did your party go, Izzie?"

Izzie didn't answer the question. "Can we talk to you, Sheila? It's important."

Sheila frowned and said, "You'd better come in."

I darted a nervous look down the path to where part of Louis's green and cream caravan was visible behind the brambles. "You're not expecting Louis, are you?"

Sheila looked at me and frowned again. "No. You two are being very mysterious. Come on in and tell me what this is all about."

We went into the kitchen and sat at the table, and it came out as garbled rubbish at first, with both Izzie and I trying to tell the story.

Sheila put up her hands to stop us. "Wait. Wait. Let me get this straight. You think that Louis is involved in wildlife smuggling on the island. And you believe this because of something the Wildlife policeman said, when you found him on the beach. You think he was talking about my van and the fact that Louis works in the Viking Hotel?" She'd opened a packet of Quality Street and offered them to us.

She made a snorting noise with her lips and said, "I'm sorry, kids, I have to say that's all a bit far-fetched. I heard that the poor man was barely conscious. I'm sure anything he said was pure nonsense. Besides, if Louis was up to anything illegal, I'd know about it. He lives at the bottom of my garden, for goodness sake. Now, I've a surgery in twenty minutes so if you don't mind ..."

This wasn't working out the way I'd hoped and I could hear the irritation in Izzie's voice when she jumped up and said, "Stealing Octavia isn't far-fetched. Louis stole my tarantula. He had her in his caravan."

I'll always remember the look on Sheila's face when Izzie said that. She was furious. I saw a vein in her neck pulse with anger.

"He *stole* the tarantula? *Stole* it?"

"Yes." Izzie was pleased with the reaction. "He stole her from my zoo. He forced the padlock on the door, broke in and took her, tank and all."

"And where is this tarantula now?"

"We um ..." I realized I was on difficult ground, "We took her back. We couldn't go to Izzie's uncle or anyone because we're not supposed to have her. If Quincy could remember, he'd help but ..." I helped myself to another Quality Street.

"And it's still alive?" Sheila almost spat the words. I was surprised she was so quite so angry seeing as it wasn't her tarantula he had stolen. "Leave this to me. I'll sort it out once and for all. I take it no one else knows about this?"

"No," we said together.

"And definitely no one else knows that you have this tarantula?"

"Only you and Quincy ... and he doesn't remember ... and now Louis."

"I'll take care of this," Sheila said getting up.

"I'm sure you're wrong about the wildlife smuggling but I'll see Louis about your spider. He won't go near it again, I promise."

Izzie was happy and almost bounced along the road as we walked back home. But there was still something bothering me. Something wasn't quite right but I couldn't figure out what it was. Mum's Clio was pulling up outside Oz Cottage so we went in.

"I've got a present for you," Mum told Izzie and gave her a book on digital photography. " I thought you might like it. You seemed so interested."

"I am … this is great. Thank you, Marissa. I bet you've got loads of baby pictures of Jack."

"I've got one right here," Mum said, opening her purse.

"Oh, please," I rolled my eyes.

Izzie leaned forward to examine the photo. "And is that Jack's dad?" I heard a roaring noise in my ears and my heart began to race in my chest. "Jack says he's working in Dubai, which is why he can't be here with you."

Mum's face blurred but I knew she'd turned to me in horror.

"But Izzie," she said, "Surely Jack's told you … his dad is dead. He died six months ago."

I don't remember opening the door. I just remember running, running, running …

11. Up-Helly-Aa

His dad is dead. His dad is dead. His dad is dead. The words pounded in my brain and beat time to my footsteps. I ran and the rain lashed at my face, stinging and burning my skin. I was glad. I wanted it to rain … hard. I wanted the wind to howl and lash the sea against the cliffs. I wanted to keep running until I couldn't run anymore.

When the stabbing pain in my side forced me to stop, I realized I was at Clickimin Broch. It looked different; darker and colder, the sky grey behind it and the tower black with rain. The earthy wet smell was strong.

I gasped for breath, each lungful of air hard and painful. I found a corner and, with my back against the damp rocks, crouched down, angry and shivering. *His dad is dead. No,* I thought at last, *"My" dad is dead.*

I don't know how long I stayed there, screwed up into a tight ball of rage. My throat ached and jagged edges of rock dug into my shoulders. I couldn't feel the cold anymore or hear the wind. My hands clenched into tight fists inside my pockets. *My dad is dead.*

If I hadn't recognized Izzie's red and yellow hoodie, I would have recognized her wild hair. Calmly, she walked the curve of the wall and squatting close beside me, pulled her hood up and huddled deep into her coat.

"Go away."

"I was hoping I'd find you here."

"I *said* … go away."

Izzie didn't reply or move. The wind howled through the tunnels of the broch, changing sound as it gusted first one way and then the other.

We sat in silence.

I was the first to speak. "Did she tell you how he died? Hey? Did she tell you how my clever father died?"

She still didn't answer.

"He fell down a hole. He was on a ship in Dubai and they'd ripped up part of the deck to fix something. Only no one had put up warning signs or fenced it off. It was dark and he fell down the hole into the hold and was killed. Just like that. Gone."

Izzie stayed silent. I could only see the side of her face but she was staring straight ahead. Not even glancing at me.

When she finally spoke it startled me. She said, "Your Mum says you wouldn't go to his funeral."

"No. Why should I? He shouldn't have died. He shouldn't have died in such a stupid way. He shouldn't have left me."

We were quiet again. I listened to the wind changes and the steady drip of the rain off the rocks.

"In January," Izzie said, "here in Lerwick, we have a fire festival called Up-Helly-Aa, to celebrate our Viking past. Thousands of people come to watch."

"So?"

"For months before, the men make a galley ... a ship like the Vikings used."

"So what?" I bit at a piece of skin by my nail until it bled.

"It's a beautiful thing. The masthead is a silver dragon, its mouth is blood red with teeth gleaming along its jaws. At the stern, the back of the boat, is the spiky tail and fins of a sea creature."

Izzie's voice was so soft that I found myself leaning forward to catch what she was saying.

"Along the sides of the galleys are Viking shields and the boat flies the banner of the black raven; the symbol of Viking rule. At about seven o'clock we switch the lights off all over Lerwick. Then we light the fire torches."

The wind dropped suddenly and with it the cutting cold.

"Men, dressed like Vikings, wearing capes and shining, winged helmets, march the galley through the streets, followed by hundreds and hundreds of other men in amazing costumes, all carrying their fire torches. Lots of the costumes are funny. Unca Dunc was a fat ballerina this year and dad was a huge baby being pushed in his pram. He even had a huge jelly dummy. I don't know where he got that from." She laughed to herself. "We have a brass band playing and everyone sings as loud as they can. The small kids are all kitted up like little Vikings too, with cardboard axes and homemade hats. They get so excited," she laughed again. "Well we all do. It's the singing and the flames swirling in the dark. It even smells exciting; like a hundred bonfires."

Izzie's words painted such a brilliant picture I could see it and almost smell the smoke of the torches. I even began to feel her excitement.

"When the galley's been carried around for a while, it's put down in the school playground, and the long, long line of men begins to circle around it. They spiral round it, their torches held high as they shout and sing. That's the bit I like best, those torches of fire, circling, round and round. Then *whoosh!* A flare is shot into the air. That's the signal for the men to throw the torches into the galley. The ship catches fire and in minutes the magnificent galley is a swirling mass of flames and we cheer and clap and …"

Izzie stopped and, for a minute, I think she was back at the fire festival. Then she shivered and for the first time since she'd sat down she looked right at me.

"It's like a Viking funeral. The Vikings burned their dead heroes in boats, and the burning galleys were floated out to sea. A good way to say goodbye to someone special, don't you think?"

I nodded, the picture of the flaming galley, floating away, bright in my mind.

Izzie put her hand in her pocket, pulled something out and held it on her open palm. It was one of the small boats, the galleys, that her dad put into the light bulbs. For a second I didn't understand.

"I have matches, too," she said, quietly. She dropped them onto the grass beside me, got up and walked towards the tower, leaving me on my own.

I stood up and left the shelter of the broch. I

felt like I was sleepwalking; everything moved in slow motion. As I drew closer to the water's edge I knew, if I did this, it would make Dad's death real. I wouldn't be able to pretend anymore.

"My dad is dead," I whispered.

My hands were shaking, but not from the cold, as I placed the little boat near the water of the loch. The wind was just a low murmur.

I struck a match, shielded it for a second and then dropped it onto the galley. I struck another and another until the boat caught fire. With a stone, I pushed it gently onto the loch. It floated for a while; a bright speck on the dark water. The strings and the banner caught and at last the tiny dragon masthead shrivelled under the flame as it bobbed further from the edge, away from me.

"Bye, dad," I whispered. "I love you." Through hot tears I watched the galley list to one side. A breeze swirled the flames into a last dance before it sank beneath the water.

I curled into myself, my arms around my knees and my head held tight to my chest and cried like I'd never stop crying again.

When I felt strong enough to stand, I found Izzie just a little way off, waiting for me.

"I expect Mum was worried when I ran out like that," I sniffed and rubbed at my nose.

She nodded. "You should go home now."

We walked over the moor together, not saying a word, but I felt so much better; kind of lighter. I wanted to talk to Mum. I wanted to talk to her about Dad and I wanted to tell her about the Viking funeral.

Mum was waiting on the doorstep. She wrapped a warm towel around me and hugged me into it. The tears started again but it didn't hurt so much and when I felt her sobbing too, I hugged her back.

Izzie slipped away to her own house.

We'd brought two chairs outside and, with blankets wrapped around us against the cold, were sitting watching the sea and sipping cups of soup.

I couldn't describe the Up-Helly-Aa fire festival anywhere near as well as Izzie had but Mum got the idea. When I told her about my Viking funeral for Dad she held her breath, listening to every word.

"He would have loved that, Jack. That's quite some friend you've made here."

"I know."

It was a whole evening of conversations starting with, "Do you remember when Dad ..." We cried some more but we laughed too.

"I think this place has a touch of magic about it," Mum said. "I'm glad we came here, aren't you?"

It was late when I heard a noise coming from Izzie's garden. It sounded like someone talking so, while mum got us another cup of soup each. I edged past the prickly bush to see if it was Izzie.

A rustle in the tree nearby startled me. Minx jumped down and miaowed around my legs. "Go on in, crazy cat," I said. "They'll be wondering where you are."

I had a quick look around the garden but if Izzie had been there she'd gone back in again because there was no one there now.

When I got back mum handed me the soup. "What's up?"

"Nothing. I just thought I heard someone talking in the garden next door. Must have imagined it."

"That reminds me," she said, "of when you, me and Dad ..." and we were off again. There was so much to remember, so many good times and so many funny times.

We'd finished the soup and the stories for now. There would be other nights to come and other stories too. I didn't want to forget any of it.

Mum stood up and folded her blanket. "How about we go to bed now and make an early start in the morning? Tomorrow's our last day."

I knew it was. In the back of my mind I knew it was, but suddenly I didn't want to leave. So much had happened but I was sure there was more to come.

Mum read the expression on my face. "I know, Jack. I don't want to go yet either but there's work for me and school for you."

"Yeah, I know."

We picked up the chairs. But before we got indoors Shetland had yet another treat for us. It started with a glow over the horizon, then red and purple rays of light shot down from space and spread across the sky like curtains.

"That's it, isn't it? Those are your Northern Lights! Quick, Mum! get your camera."

But she didn't move; she stood watching the amazing sight with her arm around my waist. More lights formed and colours rippled down, making the sheets of light look like they were blowing in the wind.

"Mum … your camera."

But she was facing out to sea, her face glowing with happiness.

"No, Jack, no camera. This one is just for you and me."

"And Dad," I said.

"And Dad," she said.

12. Octavia's revenge

It started like most of the other days on Shetland, quiet and pleasant but it certainly didn't stay that way for long.

"It's your last day," Izzie said. "What would you like to do?"

"Dunno. Just stay here … in the cove."

"We could check out the rock pools?"

I screwed up my nose.

"Don't knock it til you've tried it. They're like different little worlds."

I couldn't shake off the feeling of not wanting to go home and the stupid thing was that I knew if I didn't cheer up, I'd spoil my last day.

We were in the shed finishing the the Izzie-zoo routine. "Karma, Bombina and Octavia will miss you," Izzie said.

"I'll miss them too," I said and at that moment I realized I actually would. To make things worse the sun was shining and it was the warmest day we'd had since we came. The sea had a real sparkle to it.

"Okay rock pools. Why not."

We were hunkered down beside a pool of clear water. "See those bits of red jelly stuck to the rocks?" Izzie said. "They're anemones … and those flowers? They're anemones too. They have about two hundred tentacles with stinging cells on them. They poison small creatures that swim past; they paralyze them and then eat them."

"What is it with you and poisonous things?" I said. "I saw a jellyfish the other day, when you were with Mum and I went for a walk. I thought it was a plastic bag at first. Look! There's another one." I pointed at the water.

Izzie laughed, "No, that *is* a plastic bag."

We found starfish and prawns and Izzie told me that a jellyfish doesn't have a heart or a brain. It's just a floating stomach.

"I've got a friend like that," I said.

Mrs Christie shouted from the house. "Izzie! I'm taking your father to the hospital for his check-up. Are you coming or are you staying here with Jack?"

"I'll stay here. See you later."

Five minutes later, Mum shouted from our house. "Jack, I've got to go into town. Are you and Izzie coming or are you staying here?"

"I'm staying here." I said.

We were so busy poking around in the rock pools that we didn't hear Sheila arrive.

"Hi," she said. "I wanted to have a chat with you two. Have you got a minute?"

She beckoned for us to follow her to a flat rock halfway up the beach. She sat on the boulder and patted the space beside her. Like two well-trained puppies we sat down.

"I was wondering about the …" she glanced over her shoulder, "the tarantula."

"Did you speak to Louis about stealing her?" Izzie said.

"Yes. He confessed to everything and said he's

very sorry and he won't go near it ever again."

There was something odd about the way she said it. Like a parent telling a child a white lie. Izzie didn't seem to notice anything though.

"Well, that's good."

Sheila was glancing over her shoulder again.

"Phew it's hot." Izzie pushed her back off her face. "Fancy a cold drink, Jack? Sheila?"

"Yes." I said.

"No," Sheila said and got up too quickly. "No, you don't need a drink." I could see she was flustered. Now Izzie noticed it as well.

"What's wrong? she asked.

And then I knew. I knew for sure and I knew if I didn't do something she'd get away with it.

"It's Octavia!" I yelled. "They're after Octavia!"

I pushed past Sheila just as she grabbed Izzie.

"Don't be a fool, come back here," Sheila shouted after me.

I was up and running as fast as I could, and into the garden with one jump, slowing down only when I saw that the shed door was open. Creeping up, I looked in and there was Louis, lifting Octavia's tank off the shelf.

"Leave her alone," I flung the door open. "You promised not to steal her again."

I'd startled him but he recovered immediately. "Steal it? It's too late for that now, kid. You should have let me keep it."

Sheila arrived with Izzie still struggling to get away from her. "Let go of me. Sheila, what are you doing? I don't understand."

"I do," I said. "Your friend, Sheila here … she's

behind the smuggling on the island. Louis is just the odd job man."

"Hey, watch it, kid." he said.

Izzie stared at Sheila with shock. "That's not true. I don't believe it. Tell him it's not true, Sheila."

"She was the only one who knew about the tarantula apart from us. Quincy couldn't tell anyone, could he? He can't remember."

"That was an accident," Louis said. "I didn't mean him to fall off the cliff. Sheila said to offer him money. I told him we would give him ten thousand if he backed off."

"Shut up, you fool," Sheila said.

"No, I won't shut up. They need to know it was an accident. He was so angry, he took a swipe at me and fell."

"And you left him there all night. You didn't even check to see if he was okay."

Part of a plan was forming in my mind and I edged towards the shed door.

"It was an accident," Louis said to me and he looked really upset.

"So why did you steal the tarantula? I edged a few inches more towards the door.

"The idiot wasn't supposed to *steal* it. He was supposed to kill it. No evidence. No police snooping around. Your uncle is no fool, Izzie, or your father either. Sooner or later they would have worked it out," Sheila said.

Izzie tore her arm away from Sheila's grasp and her expression turned from disbelief to fury.

"You! You want to kill her!"

"Izzie … I have to. You must understand. It's for the ponies. It's all for the ponies. You love the ponies too, don't you? I need the money for them."

I'd got as close as I could to the door and now I needed to make Izzie understand what I intended to do. I thought if we could get outside we could lock them in and call the police. It was a brilliant plan … I thought.

Louis suddenly turned on me. "We could have had this all over with last night, but *nooo*, you had to come sneaking over into the garden, didn't you?"

"It was you I heard last night? Who were you talking to?

"The cat." Louis said.

Sheila sighed heavily. "Let's get this over with, shall we? And I'm sorry, Izzie, but whatever you tell the police it'll be your word against ours. And I'm the respectable vet here in Lerwick and you're just a child. We'll do it as painlessly as possible, I promise."

Louis picked up the tank and Izzie wrenched herself free from Sheila's grasp and made a rush at him, which wasn't good for my plan at all. She tried to grab the tank away from him, so I grabbed it too. It was a stupid struggle and could only end in one way.

The crash of glass was deafening. Louis grabbed at his hand where a cut from the glass dripped blood down his wrist and onto the floor. Sheila was shouting again and looking to see where the tarantula had gone.

"Kill it," she shouted. "Kill it now."

I pushed Izzie out outside but she struggled against me. "Leave me. Leave me."

Pushing the bolt across, I flattened myself against the shed door. "Get the key and lock the door. Lock them in."

"No, they'll kill her." Izzie sobbed.

"She stands a better chance in there with somewhere to hide. If we lock them in we can get the police. Get the key, Izzie!"

Sheila must have heard something of what I said because the shed handle turned, slowly at first and then frantically. The door rattled in its frame.

"Quickly," I shouted to Izzie. Still crying, she scrabbled under the round stone and came up with the key of the padlock. I don't know whose hands were trembling most … Izzie's as she passed it to me, or mine as I took it.

Louis was throwing his weight against the door now and I knew there was no way the bolt would hold up against him.

My hands were slippery with sweat and I missed again and again as I tried to get the key in. At last it made a loud click.

Louis stopped banging.

Apart from Izzie crying there was silence for a few seconds.

Then Sheila's voice sounding soft and gentle, "Izzie? Izzie, open the door, sweetie. We can work this out, if you just open the door."

"Phone the police," I said. "Call your Uncle Duncan."

Sheila's voice changed in an instant. "Izzie? Do

you want to hear the squish when we drop something heavy on your spider? Open the door. Now."

"No ... please don't," Izzie made a grab for the key but I held her off.

"They'll kill her anyway. Get the police." I was afraid to go myself because I was sure that the minute my back was turned Izzie would let them out. It seemed like an impossible situation and there was another few seconds of silence, like a stand-off.

Then Louis's shout, "There it is. Down there ... in the corner."

"Aha." That was Sheila again. "We've found it ... come here pretty, pretty, pretty."

"*No!*" Izzie sobbed.

There was a sudden and terrible scream from inside the shed. "My eyes!" It was Sheila. "*My eyes!*"

And then another scream, but this time the scream of a police siren as Duncan and three police officers slammed to a halt on the road outside.

In seconds they were in control, but the minute the shed door was unlocked Louis made a bolt for freedom. He caught the men unawares and pushed past them leaping over the rocks and across the beach. One PC raced after him as Duncan talked into his radio. "We need an ambulance ... Oz Cottage ... now."

Sheila was being led out still whimpering, "My eyes, my eyes ..."

"Where's this tarantula?" Duncan said.

Izzie pointed into the shed, "But she's probably dead."

It looked like this was the first the other policeman had heard about a tarantula because he almost pulled Sheila over in his hurry to get out of the way.

"I'll look," Izzie said, "It's alright," and walked into her Izzie-zoo.

"Sir, you can't let a child ..."

"This child I can," Duncan said.

There was one more scream that day, from Izzie and it was a scream of joy.

"She's alive. She's *alive.*"

Sheila was led away to the ambulance, still in pain, and holding her hands over her streaming eyes.

The PC who had chased Louis, came back out of breath, but smiling. "He out ran me, Sir, but I've put out a radio call with all the relevant information. We should have him in a few minutes. Anyone who uses a van covered with cartoon horses as a getaway car has to be an idiot."

"What happened to Sheila's eyes?" I asked Izzie.

"Octavia happened to her eyes," Izzie said. "When a tarantula is cornered it will rise up on its back legs and flick stinging hairs off its belly into a predator's eyes."

"Cool," I said.

We were both still shaken by what had happened but it was worse for Izzie. "I know she was your friend ..."

"I don't want to talk about it just yet, Jack," she said.

We got the rest of the story several hours later when Mr and Mrs Christie came back from the hospital and Mum was there too. We were outside on the Christies' patio again. Mrs Christie served up slices of lemon meringue pie onto yellow pottery plates and kept repeating, "Sheila Voss. I can't believe it, Sheila Voss."

Quincy's memory had come back, and he had immediately called Duncan and given him the whole story. Louis had been kind enough to give away Sheila's involvement when he tried to bribe him.

"I think you almost caught her in the act once," Duncan said to Mum. "When you ran out of petrol and flagged her down? She had a whole pile of scorpions in the van that time. They met their contacts at The Viking. Quincy always knew that Louis was involved somehow."

"Another slice, Duncan? So what's going to happen to those ponies of hers?" asked Mrs Christie.

"I'll look after them … at least I'll try." Izzie said.

"And just how are you going to do that?" Mrs Christie sniffed. "The poor things won't even have a field to live in soon."

"I'm betting you could do something about that, Denise." Mr Christie held out his plate and Mrs Christie slid another piece of pie onto it. "You could talk Magnus into letting us keep the ponies on that land … free of charge maybe. He's always had a soft spot for you."

Mrs Christie swiped her hand playfully over the

top of Mr Christie's head, but I could see she was pleased.

"It's not like he needs the money. He did alright from that horde of Viking silver they dug up in his top field last year," Duncan added.

"It would be for a good cause, Mum. You know how great you are at fundraising and stuff."

At the word 'fundraising' Mrs Christie's eyes lit up. "I could organize some events, I suppose, and write an article or two for *The Shetland News*. Hmm … I just need to make a few phone calls. If you'll excuse me …"

Izzie and her dad smiled at each other and did a high five.

"I'd better be off too," Duncan said. "This smuggling buisness'll mean plenty of paperwork down at the station. I wouldn't be surprised if Quincy gets a commendation for this little lot. Not that he'll want one. He's just made up that they've been caught and won't be harming any more animals. Oh, he says to say goodbye, Jack. He'll be in touch. Just as well his memory came back when it did, though. It was a close run thing, wasn't it, kids?"

I had a mouthful of meringue and couldn't speak so I just nodded. Izzie didn't answer either. I think she was still too overwhelmed by everything that had happened.

"And as for your tarantula … that was the only survivor of dozens when Louis tried to sneak one out of a box. It bit him and he dropped the lot over the side. The rest drowned, so it was one lucky spider, wasn't it?"

"Tarantula? What tarantula?" Mrs Christie had returned unseen and was instantly alarmed. Panic widened her eyes.

Duncan pulled a face. "Ah, well I'd better to get back to the station. I'll leave that explanation for you then shall I, Izzie? Go easy with her, Denise, it's been a hard day and these two have been through a lot."

"What tarantula? "Mrs Christie was getting annoyed.

"Jack?" Izzie's eyes pleaded.

"I'm sorry, Izzie, I've got to go pack." I sighed, "and I have some explaining of my own to do."

"What tarantula?" Mrs Christie said again.

We were at the ferry port for six and had a long wait while the cars filed on one by one. The Christies, including Duncan, had come to wave us off. I managed a few words alone with Izzie, who was looking very sorry for herself.

"What's going to happen about Octavia?"

She blew out between her lips. "It's going to be an uphill struggle, but Dad, Duncan and Quincy are on my side. Between the four of us we *might* stand a chance. I'll email you. What about you? Did you get into much trouble for hiding a spider?"

"Two weeks no telly, computer games or iPod. I'll survive. If I practise hard, I might even get to master *Twinkle, Twinkle, Little Star* on my guitar." That brought a smile to her face. "So, I guess I'll see you then."

"Aye, see you."

"I'll wave from up on deck."

"Okay."

Once we'd crawled into the belly of the ferry, parked the Clio, unpacked what we needed for the night and found our cabin, I went up on deck.

Good old Lerwick had sent a nice cold wind to see us off and Mum's face was half hidden by a big woolly scarf. I hunched over and pulled my hood up. The railing was too cold to hold onto.

The Christies seemed a fair way off from up on deck but I would have spotted Izzie's hair anywhere. We waved and they waved back. When the ferry eventually started with that big engine thrust, I felt a strange mixture of feelings. It had been the best holiday ever but in some ways it had been the worst.

"I guess we'll come back next year?" I said.

"Oh, we'll be back next year for sure. Maybe even before that if the magazine wants more pictures."

We waved again. With a tremble right through the ship we began to sail away from Lerwick and the Shetlands.

We stayed on deck waving until we couldn't see them any more and then I headed straight for our cabin. I was feeling really sick.